The last thing Charlie Fox expected, when she headed out on routine patrol that day, was to end up riding into a firefight, on horseback, with the Spice Girls...

Charlie Fox is one of the toughest cookies you could ever hope to meet. A word of advice—don't try to get her to talk about her time in the military. Let's just say it didn't end well.

But before her fall from grace, Charlie was considered a rising star. She made it through one of the toughest challenges any soldier would have to face—Selection for Special Forces. The nightmare that came next is a story I've explored in scenes and flashbacks throughout the series.

But what happened *before* that? Back when Charlie was a young soldier in the regular army, on patrol in Afghanistan, being kept away from the front line fighting as stipulated by the regulations concerning female personnel. What did she do back then to prove her worth as a specialised soldier, under life-and-death conditions? How did she earn her chance?

That is a story I've never told.

Until now.

"I highly recommend this series!"

— BESTSELLING AUTHOR, IAN RANKIN

"Male and female crime fiction readers alike will find Sharp's writing style addictively readable."

— PAUL GOAT ALLEN, *CHICAGO TRIBUNE*

"Scarily good."

— BESTSELLING AUTHOR, LEE CHILD

"Whenever I turn the first page on a Charlie Fox novel, I know that her creator is going to serve up a complex, fast-paced military-grade action romp than can hold its head high in the male-dominated thriller world."

— LINDA WILSON, *CRIME REVIEW UK*

"Zoë Sharp is one of the sharpest, coolest, and most intriguing writers I know. She delivers dramatic, action-packed novels with characters we really care about."

— BESTSELLING AUTHOR, HARLAN COBEN

"This is hard-edged fiction at its best."

— MICHELE LEBER, *BOOKLIST* STARRED REVIEW FOR FIFTH VICTIM

"Superb."

— KEN BRUEN, BESTSELLING AUTHOR OF THE JACK TAYLOR SERIES, THE GUARDS, BLITZ

"If you don't like Zoë Sharp there's something wrong with you. Go and live in a cave and get the hell out of my gene pool! There are few writers who go right to the top of my TBR pile—Zoë Sharp is one of them."

— BESTSELLING AUTHOR, STUART MACBRIDE

"Every book in this suspenseful series opens with a scene that grabs the reader by the throat and doesn't let go until the final page... Sharp creates some of the best action sequences in fiction... Don't miss out on one of the best thriller writers around."

— TED HERTEL JR, *DEADLY PLEASURES MYSTERY MAGAZINE*

"The bloody bar fights are bloody brilliant, and Charlie's skills are formidable and for real."

— MARILYN STASIO, *NEW YORK TIMES*, ON **KILLER INSTINCT**

"What I love about this series is the fact that Zoë Sharp pulls the reader into every scenario—creates a world where you are part of the action and then leaves you gasping for breath as the final conclusion comes around. It's a total experience and one I look forward to each and every time!"

— NOELLE HOLTEN, *CRIME BOOK JUNKIE*

"Charlotte 'Charlie' Fox is one of the most vivid and engaging heroines ever to swagger onto the pages of a book. Where Charlie goes, thrills follow."

— BESTSELLING AUTHOR, TESS GERRITSEN, AUTHOR OF THE RIZZOLI & ISLES SERIES

TRIAL UNDER FIRE

PREQUEL TO THE CHARLIE FOX SERIES

ZOË SHARP

First published in Great Britain 2021
ZACE

Registered UK Office:
128 City Road, London EC1V 2NX
zace.ltd@gmail.com

ISBN-13: 978-1-909344-42-6
ISBN-10: 1-909344-42-7

For all those who were there

ALSO BY ZOË SHARP

the Charlie Fox thrillers

KILLER INSTINCT: #1

RIOT ACT: #2

HARD KNOCKS: #3

CHARLIE FOX: THE EARLY YEARS (eBooks 1,2,3)

FIRST DROP: #4

ROAD KILL: #5

SECOND SHOT: #6

CHARLIE FOX: BODYGUARD (eBooks 4,5,6)

THIRD STRIKE: #7

FOURTH DAY: #8

FIFTH VICTIM: #9

DIE EASY: #10

ABSENCE OF LIGHT: #11

FOX HUNTER: #12

BAD TURN: #13

TRIAL UNDER FIRE: prequel

FOX FIVE RELOADED: short story collection

the CSI Grace McColl & Detective Nick Weston

Lakes crime thrillers

DANCING ON THE GRAVE: #1

BONES IN THE RIVER: #2

standalone crime thrillers

THE BLOOD WHISPERER

AN ITALIAN JOB (with John Lawton)

the Blake & Byron mystery thrillers

THE LAST TIME SHE DIED

For Behind the Scenes, Bonus Features, Freebies, Sneak Peeks and advance notice of new releases, sign up for Zoë's **VIP list** at **www.ZoeSharp.com/vip-mailing-list**.

AUTHOR'S NOTE

As an author, I *hugely* appreciate all the feedback, reviews, and ratings my books receive from my readers. It helps others make an informed decision before they buy. If you enjoy this book, please consider leaving a brief review or a rating on goodreads or on the retailer site where you made your purchase.
Links can be found at **www.ZoeSharp.com**.
THANK YOU!

1

THE PAIR of helos came in low and dark over the ravine. One minute they were a faint whump-whump in the distance, the next they were right on top of us. Two sudden, snarling silhouettes, each big as a truck, blotting out the stars. The downdraft from the rotors thrashed the dusty scrub around us. I dropped flat onto the rock with lips and eyelids clamped shut, rolling my rifle under me to the keep the worst of the grit out of the moving parts.

As it settled, Tate cautiously lifted his head, spat out a mouthful of sand.

"What the fuck was that?" he demanded. "D'you think Ana's mum knows she's out this late, giving us a look-see up her skirts?"

"That wasn't Ana," I said, and we both knew I was talking about the ANA—the Afghan National Army. "Not unless they've scrapped those old Russian Mils. That was a pair of Lynx. Ours."

"You sure?" After a moment he snorted at his own question. "Yeah. 'Course you are."

I ignored him, went up the nearest slope in a fast crawl and peered over the rim. The helicopters were halfway down the valley by then, still hugging the terrain as they crested the next rise and dropped from view.

"Think we ought to call it in?"

I threw him a dirty look he failed to catch. "They're not showing lights and if they were any lower they'd be driving not flying. The last thing those lads want is us blabbing their position." *Or ours, come to that.*

I didn't mention the fact that, although I was the unit's signaller, in charge of comms, according to the letter of the rules I wasn't supposed to be out in a possible combat zone on a night patrol, routine or not.

The Powers That Be were funny about putting us 'lumpy jumpers'—one of the more acceptable nicknames by which female personnel were known—in the firing line. I'd handled enough radio traffic for incoming wounded back at Camp Bastion to be partly grateful for that.

And partly frustrated as hell.

What was the point in being a soldier if I was never asked to fight?

"Even so," Tate said, "maybe we need to—"

Whatever he'd been about to say was cut off by the initial crack and streaking whine of an RPG fired way forward of our position, somewhere to the northeast. We both ducked, flinching. Tate swore.

By the time I looked up, the rocket motor had already ignited after launch. The slight wobble corrected as the fins deployed—the smaller front set inducing a stabilising rotational spin. It appeared for all the world like a rogue firework as it arced over the horizon on an intercept course with the helos.

Compared to the rapid spit of tracer fire, the RPG's slow muzzle velocity, less than three hundred metres a second, made it seem to fly almost lazily, trailing a short comet flare behind it.

I grabbed for the mic pressel on the Bowman Command Net Radio and yelled, "RPG incoming!" in the hope that the helo pilots were monitoring the standard frequencies as well as mission-specific.

There was a breathless pause. Long enough for me to think that maybe—just maybe—they had time for evasive manoeuvres.

But *not* long enough for that to actually happen.

The night sky erupted with an intense ball of white-hot flame, turning a dirty orange with burning smoke. A second or so later the thunder-crack of the explosion rolled over us.

"Holy crap," Tate muttered. "Poor bastards."

Movement farther back in the ravine had both of us squirming round, weapons readied.

"Easy, lads." Our patrol leader, Captain MacLeod, dropped onto his elbows between us. He, at least, was gender-blind when it came to addressing his troops. We were all "lads" to him. "Let's have a sit-rep."

I tuned out Tate's explanation, too busy trying to patch together a better picture of the situation from the fractured voices on the net.

Captain MacLeod flicked his eyes to me. He wasn't a big guy, but he was solid and fast on his feet, fair-haired, with pale skin that went pink in the fierce Afghan sun without ever tanning, despite copious applications of sunblock. His family background —one of the better parts of Edinburgh—was evident in his voice, even though his accent had been further rounded off by public school, where I heard he'd terrorised opposing teams on the rugby pitch.

"How bad?"

"One helo down for certain," I said. "They've got serious casualties and are taking incoming fire."

"Damn. See if you can get their position. Contact brigade HQ for an immediate casevac. Advise that we'll move up to provide tactical support, and secure an HLZ. But don't mention—"

"—the second helo unless they do it first," I finished for him. "Yes, sir."

He grinned. "All right, Charlie. Not everyone loves a smart-arse, eh?"

"No, sir."

He slapped me on the shoulder hard enough to sting and scrambled backwards down into the ravine.

Tate stayed alongside, scanning the terrain through his night-vision goggles. I got on the net to our brigade headquarters, mentally working up an approximate grid reference for the crash site as I did so. In the near-distance, we could hear automatic weapons fire and see the occasional spit of tracers against the absolute black.

Even as I carried out my orders, I had a feeling I'd be one of those waiting on the stretch of ground we cleared as a Helicopter Landing Zone, rather than getting into the thick of a skirmish with local Taliban. I wasn't sure whether to be relieved or disappointed by that.

A moment later, Captain MacLeod was back with our medic, a lanky corporal called Brookes.

"Both helos are down," I told them. "The RPG took out the first bird, and they think shrapnel from the explosion may have forced the second to make an emergency landing."

"MERT on its way?" MacLeod asked.

"Yes, sir. Brigade's sending a Chinook from Bastion."

Brookes was frowning. "What do we know about casualties?"

"In the first Lynx there are two dead, one Cat-A wounded, and two Cat-Bs." I said. "I haven't been able to make contact with the second Lynx."

The British Army designates wounded by three categories from A—in need of immediate surgery—to C—safe to patch up in the field. The only thing we could do with Cat-Bs was stabilise them long enough to get them back to the main hospital at Camp Bastion where they would be worked on by some of the best trauma surgeons in the business.

Brookes gave one of his deceptively cheery smiles. "Sounds like we'd best get over there a bit sharpish then, hadn't we?"

My eyes flicked to MacLeod. He looked up from checking my grid references, frowning, as if he didn't know why I hesitated.

"You heard Corporal Brookes. We've got a lot of ground to cover and I need decent comms when we get there. So get your arse into gear, soldier!"

2

My parents did not take it well when I announced I was joining up. Maybe if I'd been the son my father always wanted, things might have been different.

Maybe a lot of things would have been different.

I can still remember breaking the news to them at home in Cheshire, over one of the excruciatingly formal Sunday lunches of which my mother was so fond. For a few moments after my bald statement of intent, the only sound in the room was the mournful tick of the long-case clock in the corner.

Then my mother let her soup spoon drop into her bowl with something approaching a clatter.

"Oh, *Charlotte,*" she murmured. "But it's so…so *unsuitable,* darling."

"Why?" I demanded, feeling my temper start to rise even though I'd promised myself it wouldn't—that this was precisely the reaction I'd expected. "Anybody would think I'd told you I was going into prostitution."

"There's no need to be vulgar, Charlotte," she said primly. "Surely you can understand our…reservations about such a career choice."

I noted her collective term and glanced at my father. He, too, had stopped spooning his soup at my announcement. Silently, he began to eat again, with the same mechanical precision he applied to his surgical work. The spoon angled just so, the amount of soup in each mouthful exactly equal to the last mil. I could imagine you'd spot his professional handiwork at first glance by the symmetry of the stitches.

Not that high-ranking consultant orthopaedic surgeons closed their own incisions anymore—they probably had minions for that.

"Do you have an opinion you'd care to voice?" I couldn't resist poking him with the pointed stick of challenge, as if hoping that this time I might provoke a reaction. I should have known better.

"I am not prepared to discuss this over the luncheon table," he said with calm indifference. "I believe your mother has prepared roast lamb."

I flopped back in my chair. "Oh, well, if the cut of the meat is more important than my future, let's not, by all means."

My mother made a flutter of protest, but he silenced both of us with a single barbed glance over his glasses, and carried on with his soup.

He could be bloody-minded like that, my father.

Maybe that was where I got it from.

But after our empty plates were cleared away, and I'd dutifully helped stack the dishwasher, and wiped down the surfaces, I took him coffee in his study and closed the door behind me once I was inside.

It was an austere room, all dark green leather and beeswaxed oak. He sat behind his desk like a hanging judge and waited for me to state my case. I stuffed my hands in the back pockets of my jeans, nervous, and irritated that he was the cause of it.

"I think it's something I might be rather good at," I said without preamble.

"How so?"

"Well, I can shoot."

That had been a chance discovery on an outward bound course. The instructors had told me I was a natural—that I had an instinctive feel for a target. In fact, it was only when I tried to analyse what I was doing that my shots began to go wild. If I just relaxed into it, I nailed the bulls-eye every time.

My father waited for me to elaborate, but I'd been lured into that trap too often to fall this time. I said nothing. I dragged the chair that faced his desk off to one side slightly, turned it at an angle so this felt less like an inquisition, and sat.

Eventually, he sighed, picked up his coffee and took a measured sip.

"I have been known to accept the occasional invitation to a day on the grouse moor myself," he said then. "It's something one does as a hobby, or for sport. That's no reason to want to make a career out of it."

I didn't immediately respond to that. How did I admit that it was the first time anything had seemed to come naturally to me?

I knew without conceit that I was bright, but recognised I lacked true academic engagement. My mother had cajoled me into dance and music lessons, which had bored me rigid. I'd been decent enough in Pony Club competitions, had made my mark in junior hunter trials and three-day events, but wasn't sure I had the outright passion to take it to any kind of higher level. I was physically fit, but not in the running for any medals.

"Well, since *you* have all the answers, what do *you* think I ought to do?" I demanded, weariness making my tone more sarcastic than it might otherwise have been. "Take a shorthand typing course and hope to flash my legs at some ambitious young salesman so he puts a ring on my finger, then move to a nice semi in Swindon, and spawn you a couple of grandkids?"

He paused a moment, as if pointedly making sure I was quite finished, before he put down his cup.

"Leaving aside your apparent capabilities with a firearm for just one moment," he said. "What exactly do you hope to get out of signing up for the military?"

I swallowed. *Respect. A sense of belonging, of not being some kind of cuckoo child shoved into the wrong nest, of finally fitting inside my own skin.*

And I knew without a doubt I couldn't voice any of that to him.

"I think it's an opportunity to do something worthwhile," I said instead.

He linked his hands together on the desktop. He had short,

pristine nails at the tips of fingers that were almost slender, their only adornment a plain gold wedding ring.

"One of my former colleagues was asked some time ago to consult for the Ministry of Defence on the suitability of women in more active military roles," he said. "After exhaustive enquiries, his conclusion was that female soldiers possess neither the mental nor physical resilience required to serve alongside their male counterparts on the front line."

Never one to sugar the pill either, my father. I could only be thankful he'd never become an oncologist. If he handed out cancer diagnoses with such blunt candour, his patients would have left in droves.

"I hate to break this to you, but women are no longer regarded as second-class citizens," I snapped back. "We even have the *vote* now and everything."

The muscle in his cheek gave the smallest twitch, hardly visible, but which for him indicated major irritation.

"I hardly think that the Chiefs of Staff will take into account a desire for gender equality driven by petty political correctness, at the expense of this country's preparedness for combat."

"So, because I may not be allowed to actually stand in the trenches, you think I should give up on the whole idea? There's more to an army career than just being a squaddie."

He tilted his head slightly, regarded me with cool detachment. "But you've just based your entire argument, such as it was, on your ability to shoot. If you want to achieve success in the military channels that *are* open to you, Charlotte, you'd have to excel at those very administrative tasks to which you have just referred with such disdain."

"If that's the case, what does it matter if I do the job in the army or in civvy street?"

"Because at least, as a civilian, you won't be required to sign a binding contract for a minimum period of four years' service."

I rose, a buzzing in my ears now, a tightness in my hands. "So, what it boils down to is, you don't think I can hack it."

He glanced at the empty chair as if to emphasise my lack of self-control.

"Quite frankly, no. I don't believe you can," he said with

lethal calm, and picked up his copy of the *Financial Times* as though that was the end of the matter.

He let me get halfway to the door. "Oh, and Charlotte?"

"Yes?"

"Do please let your mother know when you're likely to be home on leave, won't you? Then she can ensure your room will be ready."

I didn't respond to that, although I did manage not to slam the door off its frame as I went out. And the following morning, I walked into the nearest army recruiting office determined to prove him wrong.

3

In military parlance, TAB stands for Tactical Advance to Battle. To a squaddie on the ground, it means hoofing it as fast as your hairy little legs will carry you.

Right now, my patrol was tabbing it towards the location of the downed helo with as much speed as we could manage, at night, over terrain that was hostile both in terms of topography and demographic.

Truth be told, we were ill-equipped to conduct a rescue mission under fire. The ten-man patrol was doing little more than a wide perimeter sweep from our Forward Operating Base in the Nawa-I-Barakzayi district of Helmand province. We were travelling at night to try to catch some sign of the Taliban who'd been making regular attacks on two other FOBs in the vicinity.

Creatures of habit, they tended to use the tried and tested strategy of an attack at last light, knowing they had the advantage of familiarity with every escape route or trail in the surrounding area—including any that we might use.

The terrain was severe enough that our vehicles had been shaking themselves to pieces if we tried to push on. And they disintegrated twice as fast if we tried to push on in the dark, when it was so much harder to avoid the larger rocks and treacherous ravines. Seen through the eerie green cast of our night-vision gear, it looked like the surface of the moon, only not quite so hospitable. It had reached the stage where the lads were having to carry out repairs to the suspension and steering of our Land Rovers after every recce.

Hence this exploratory night foot patrol, with a purely watch-and-learn remit. A small group, travelling relatively light, with just enough armament to cover our retreat, should we need to make one.

But not enough to secure an advance, or to extract casualties under fire.

Still, improvisation was the name of the game, and Captain MacLeod was the kind of officer who'd gone out of his way to forge a decent relationship with those under his command. As I stumbled along in the dark, trying not to clog my lungs with the fine dust that coated everything, I think we all had enough confidence to follow him anywhere.

Unlike *his* boss, our OC, who seemed to go out of his way to keep any female soldiers so far out of the firing line we may as well never have left the recruit training camp in Guildford.

We didn't need to ask how much farther it was to our objective. Not only could I see the burning Lynx in the distance, but now I could smell it with every breath, too.

The Westland Lynx is constructed using a high percentage of magnesium alloy components. A material that's great for its light weight, low density, and durability at high operating temperatures, it forms a major part of the transmission and main rotor gearbox casings. The downside is, it burns. And when it burns, it stinks of ammonia.

Combined with the greasy smoke from the aviation kerosene, it must have been noticeable for miles around. Afghanistan is not exactly troubled by light pollution. So that meant if we were locked in on the giant distress flare, so was everybody else in the vicinity.

And I doubted many of them were friendly.

Already, we could hear the crisp smack of NATO rounds going down, against the deeper rattle of AK fire. The air was filled with the zip and sizzle that high-velocity rounds make as they pass way too close for comfort.

We slowed our approach, covering our flanks as MacLeod

and his sergeant worked out a rough plan. Sergeant Clarke was a thickset guy whose parents had come over from Jamaica in the 1960s, when he was still a babe in arms. He'd grown up with a Home Counties accent, but with enough beer inside him, his party piece was to spout fluent Yardie.

I hunched over the Bowman CNR, trying to patch in to whatever frequency the covert team were using.

"Any luck, Charlie?"

"Negative, sir. I had them, but I've lost them again. I think maybe their comms have given out."

"Bugger it. Keep trying anyway."

"Yes, sir."

The Bowman had not long come into service and the bugs in the system were legendary, to the point where most squaddies swore it stood for Better Off With Map And Nokia. Still, we were all equipped with our Personal Role Radio, or PRR, which had an operating range of around 500 metres.

Sergeant Clarke recce'd forwards with two of the lads, soon reporting that the Lynx had gone down hard into a natural bowl intersected by another ravine. The survivors had apparently found minimal cover, but were pinned down.

The enemy had the high ground on the north side, where they had uninterrupted fields of fire in both directions along the ravine, and a clear view of the south slope to prevent any attempt at a retreat. In any case, falling back that way involved a hundred-metre dash up a steep incline covered with scrubby vegetation and rocks not big enough to hide a rat behind. It was a recipe for getting shot in the back.

The only thing in the downed team's favour was the burning Lynx, and even that was a double-edged sword. The Taliban fighters were well aware that it could go up in a big way at any moment, and without knowing what explosives or ammo might be aboard, they didn't want to risk being caught close inside the blast radius. Advancing on the men down in the bowl would bring them well within that zone. Of course, the pinned-down survivors were far too close, also, but they didn't have much of a choice in the matter.

MacLeod ordered half a dozen of our lads into position along the south lip of the ravine, making the best use of available cover, and spread out to imitate a larger force.

"Charlie, I want you and Corporal Brookes watching our rear," he said. "The last thing we need is another group of the bastards creeping up on us."

Brookes frowned. "If there are wounded, sir, I will have to leave station to deal with them."

MacLeod gave him a tense smile. "I'm well aware of that, corporal. Why do you think I've teamed you with the best shot in the unit?"

He flashed me a grin. "Good point, sir."

MacLeod waited until he'd gone and then paused next to where I knelt, arranging myself in the dirt behind the optical sight of my SA80.

"You OK there, Charlie?"

Just for a second, I wondered if he'd asked purely because I was female, then dismissed the thought. He would have checked regardless. I was—quite literally in this case—tail-end Charlie. If Brookes was called to a man down, the safety of the entire patrol lay in my hands.

"Of course, sir."

"Good lad," he murmured, as if to emphasise there was no special treatment involved, and he disappeared into the night.

4

Anybody who's ever been in a firefight will know just how chaotic it is. Not least because the adrenaline is rampaging through your system and all your senses seem to be running at maximum revs, even though I was four months into my tour in Afghanistan at that point. This was not my first time under fire by any stretch.

I took a couple of long, deep breaths, willed my heart to slow its pounding to a steadier rhythm. I knew I would never hit anything if I allowed my sight picture to be shunted all over the place by the beat of my own pulse.

As soon as our lads opened up from concealment on the south side of the ravine, the firing intensified. I shut it out of my mind, tried not to pay attention to the battle being fought behind me. I kept one eye on the image overlaid by the illuminated reticle inside the scope, and the other open in the darkness, now strobe-lit by muzzle flash.

It was unusual for the Taliban to mount a conventional military assault, or even to hold their ground when they faced a possible pitched battle with coalition forces. Guerrilla hit-and-run tactics had served them well when their countrymen were kicking the arse of the Russians during the 1980s. And they hadn't done too badly at kicking ours back in the mid-1800s, either.

So, either the crew of the Lynx was of importance, or the insurgents were waiting for something to happen…

When I caught another flash high to my left—southeast of our position—at first I took it for more weapons fire. I tracked right and left, hunting for another burst, but nothing came.

A padded knee hit the dirt near my shoulder.

"You see that, Charlie?" Corporal Brookes demanded. He had to lean in and yell in my ear to be heard over the crackle of the guns. "What d'you reckon?"

I lifted my head. "Didn't see enough of it to make a guess," I said. "Small arms, maybe? If it was another RPG, it would have hit us by now."

"Now there's a cheery thought. If you—"

"There!" I interrupted him. "There it is again. It's a vehicle—headlights, look. Coming fast, if the way they're jolting around is anything to go by."

"The mad buggers. They'll rip the axles out of that thing."

"Well, let's hope they do it sooner rather than later, then."

I dropped my face back to the scope, saw with more clarity an old Toyota pick-up truck, the rear bed crammed with Taliban fighters. They sat packed in so close their knees interlocked together, bristling with the usual AKs, but also PK machine guns, and old bolt-action Lee-Enfields.

I'd learned to make a fairly accurate estimate of distance using the mil-dots on the SA80's reticle against the size of a known object, like the ubiquitous Toyota pick-up. By my reckoning, they were already a little over 800 metres away, and closing as fast the terrain would allow.

Brookes was saying something but I'd tuned him out as I tried to relax behind the gun, to melt into the dirt beneath me. I tracked the pick-up as it bucked and rocked over the ground. Vague calculations ran through my mind as I tried to predict where the jolting front headlights would land next, rather than where they were now.

I tried to concentrate on a point directly between the lights, where I knew the front grille of the Toyota would be, and the vulnerable radiator behind that. I could see it clearly inside my head, a target maybe half a metre square. And I told myself it was easy as I squeezed the trigger.

The truck reared up at the moment I fired, so it might almost have been reacting viscerally to the shot, but I knew I'd missed. They had gained another twenty or so metres by now, still coming, still closing.

I was at the limit of the effective range of the SA80, but ever since the army had discovered the ability I had with a long gun, they'd encouraged me to put down thousands of rounds in training, to enter Skill-at-Arms meetings and the competitions held at Bisley.

And if I left it much longer, the men advancing would have us well within the range of their battered AK47s. The Lee-Enfields some of them carried dated back before the Second World War. Old, true, but in the hands of an experienced fighter they could be deadly at a greater distance.

"You're never aiming for that truck are you?" Brookes said. "'Cos you'll be bloody lucky to—"

I ignored him, fired again, a two-round burst this time as the front of the truck came down, and immediately saw from the steam hissing out into the beam of the headlights that I'd scored a hit. The driver jerked the wheel in reaction, almost overturning the vehicle. It wrenched to a stop and I caught movement as the occupants bailed out into cover, expecting my next shots to be aimed at them.

"You jammy fucker!" Brookes said, just as Captain MacLeod reappeared alongside us.

"Corporal Brookes, give us a heads-up as soon as that truck gets within—"

"Don't think they're going to get any closer, sir," Brookes said. He jerked his head in my direction. "Seems like they ran into car trouble."

As soon as their reinforcements evaporated, the Taliban pulled back, and we were able to venture down into the ravine.

The heat from the burning Lynx was intense. I could feel my

eyebrows trying to shrink back into my forehead. I realised, too, that what I could smell was not entirely mechanical. Not everyone had got out of the helo when it came down, and clearly the survivors did not have chance to retrieve the bodies before the aircraft began to burn. It made my stomach heave.

Corporal Brookes was already treating the wounded. Nobody who survived the initial crash had escaped uninjured. The pilot and co-pilot had died either on impact, or in the fire that quickly followed. One of the four-man team on board was unconscious and unresponsive. Another two had broken limbs—one a compound fracture. The final team member had hit the ground OK, but had subsequently taken a round in the gut as they made cover.

He'd kept firing, though, as had the two other conscious men, but I could see by their haggard faces in the light from the blaze what it had cost them.

I saw something else, too. None of the team wore rank or regimental insignia. It went with the unlit helos, and the apparent determination of the enemy not only to bring them down, but to finish them off once they'd done so.

Now the fear of the firefight was over, and the adrenaline hangover started to kick in, the man who'd been gut-shot discovered just how much pain he was in. He was dripping in sweat, his exposed skin glistening with far more than mere heat. He was well-spoken, a far-back accent that made the obscenities that tumbled from his mouth seem somehow more shocking but less heartfelt. I pegged him for an officer, missing pips on his shoulders notwithstanding.

Corporal Brookes shot him full of morphine and arranged him sitting with his back against a rock, propped with his knees bent up to his chest to keep what compression was possible on his abdomen.

I relayed a message in a set format, known as a nine-liner, to HQ, giving, among other things, the location and security of the evac site, category condition of the wounded, the fact they were all stretcher cases, and that we'd mark the HLZ with flares. After all, with the Lynx likely to burn until dawn, a few smaller fires in the vicinity were not going to make a vast amount of difference.

Brookes improvised stretchers for the two Cat-A wounded—the officer and the unconscious man. The two Cat-Bs had to managc using a squaddie as a support crutch, and more or less hopping on their good leg. We didn't have the manpower available for anything more. Even MacLeod hooked his shoulder under that of the guy with the compound fracture—now heavily splinted—and did his bit. I was at one side of the bivouac sheet being used for the officer, at the foot end.

We staggered up the shifting side of the ravine with grimly gritted teeth, trying to ignore the muffled yells of the wounded man.

And as soon as we crested the top, the man opposite me, a Geordie lad called Baz, dropped his side of the sheet and grabbed for his rifle.

The officer roared in pain. I was about to bollock Baz when I realised what had prompted his reaction.

In front of us, barely visible against the terrain into which they blended, I could see half a dozen rifle muzzles with dark figures behind them. And they were all aiming straight at us.

5

For a second that seemed to expand into infinity, we stared into the dangerous end of six unknown soldiers. Baz had acted quickly, but hadn't managed to do more than get a hand to his own weapon before common sense overcame training reflex and he, like the rest of us, froze.

Then the officer on the stretcher recovered his breath enough to rasp, "Hell, sergeant...you boys have been a *fucking* long time."

The men rose out of concealment in what seemed to be one fluid movement. Four of them were dressed identically to the men we carried, in combat gear devoid of badges or name tabs. The first thought that ran through my head was *Special Forces.*

The other two men were clearly flight crew. There was something just a little less predatory, a little less practised, about the way they handled the weapons they carried. Like they were used to delivering lead at a distance farther removed from brutal reality.

One of the covert team came forwards—the one the officer had identified as a sergeant, although he wore no stripes to confirm the rank. His rifle still up in his shoulder and his eyes everywhere.

"Boss," he said, voice clipped and devoid of emotion. "You're not looking too good."

"Fuck that, man. Where *were* you?"

The man jerked his head towards the darkness surrounding us. "Our bird took shrapnel when you got hit. We were lucky, but we set down about four klicks southwest of here. Had to tab in."

"Well, we're a…bust now. These lads are evac'ing…us back to base." He could hardly manage the breath to speak. "The MERT helo will be here in…how long?"

Although he didn't address the question to any of us in particular, I had the countdown clock to the arrival of the Medical Emergency Response Team running inside my head.

"Forty minutes, sir."

That made the newcomer, the sergeant, flick his eyes in my direction, but no more than that.

Without a word being said between them, the others moved in to help carry their colleagues. The sergeant stepped in close to me, reached for the corner of the bivouac sheet we were using as a sling for the officer. I held fast.

"I *can* manage."

The sergeant stilled. "Never said you couldn't," he said sharply, "but he and I need to have a chat on the way to the HLZ, so get that stick out of your arse and move over, soldier."

I relinquished my corner immediately and hurried out of his way. And I was suddenly glad of the darkness to hide the mortified flush of colour in my cheeks.

WE REACHED the Helicopter Landing Zone far enough ahead of time to be able to secure it. Captain MacLeod spread our lads out to keep a watchful eye on the perimeter. The sergeant who'd taken my place helped put down his load and went without a word to the other members of his team. I didn't know what he and the wounded officer discussed during their chat *en route,* but neither of them looked particularly happy about it.

MacLeod jogged over to me for a sit-rep.

"ETA nine minutes, sir," I said. I hesitated a moment, then nodded towards the huddle the sergeant made with his boys. "Who *are* they?"

"Far better you don't know that, Charlie," he said, and there was a tightness to his voice I'd come to both recognise and be wary of. He didn't know much, either, I gathered, and was frustrated as hell by the fact.

It wasn't entirely by chance, then, that the pair of us were still close by the wounded officer when the sergeant returned, with his team a couple of paces behind him.

"We're going to stand on," he said without preamble. "For the op."

The officer was desperately trying to move around the pain now, unable to keep still, but twisted by it when he failed to do so. His hands clutched at the side of the sheet until I thought the bones would crack through the skin. Sweat and grime coated his face, and the front of his combat jacket gleamed dark with blood.

Corporal Brookes was frowning as he pumped another morphine shot into him. I saw him catch MacLeod's eye and give a fractional shake of his head, and realised why he wasn't worried about overdosing his patient.

"Don't be fucking...stupid, man," the officer managed, more gasp than speech. "Half the team's...gone. You don't have the men...or the expertise."

"If it wasn't important, we wouldn't be here," the sergeant said. "We all of us knew this wasn't going to be an easy ride."

"You still...don't have—"

"What we haven't got, we'll borrow or steal as we go."

"No, sergeant! That's a...fucking order."

"I'll take your *order* under advisement," the sergeant said flatly. "Face it, you'll be dead before the MERT gets here. Unless you want your last act to be that of a coward, you'll order me to go on with the job and you'll go out like a fucking hero instead."

And with that he turned away and stalked into the darkness. The other three gave the officer a last blank stare, then turned and followed without a word.

He was not, I judged, one of those officers his men would have followed anywhere. The sergeant, on the other hand, could have led them to hell.

Perhaps that's where they were heading.

I kept in touch with the Chinook pilot on the way in. When

we heard the distinctive double thump of his rotors, MacLeod ordered the flares lit. We were still close enough to the burning Lynx for that to be the bigger draw, but it always ratcheted up the odds of a contact. The Chinook was at its most vulnerable for the period it was on the ground, even with a pair of AgustaWestland Apaches riding shotgun.

As the Chinook set down, we crouched as close to the landing zone as we dared, huddled over the wounded to protect them from the twin rotors' punishing downdraught. It pounded us viciously, whipping my combat jacket and shirt up so the sand grit-blasted my back.

The crew had the rear loading ramp coming down before the big helo was even on the ground. We ran out with the wounded, bent double, breath held against the powdered dirt, up into the belly of the Chinook. The rear load bay smelled of aviation turbine fuel, canvas and rubber.

Corporal Brookes did the handover to the medical personnel riding with the helo. He had to shout to be heard over the roar of engines, talking fast but clear so there'd be no confusion, no mistakes. The taut efficiency was at odds with his usual laid-back attitude. There was nobody else I'd trust to keep my heart pumping if I went down in the field.

Last man in was the wounded officer. The men from the second Special Forces team carried him, with care but no particular reverence. It was only as they loaded him in I registered that he'd stopped writhing.

Stopped moving.

Stopped breathing, too.

As they set him down, the last thing the sergeant did was flip the cover of the bivvy sheet over the officer's face. Then he jogged back down the loading ramp, even as it was starting to rise.

The Chinook lifted off quickly, rotating as it climbed, and blasting us with more dirt and grit. The pair of Apaches buzzed around it like attendant wasps, bristling with armament, ready to sting.

We pulled back fast after the helos peeled away, slipping into the darkness and leaving the flares gradually dwindling on the rocky ground.

I trotted along in MacLeod's wake as he caught up with the Special Forces team. They had formed a huddle and were taking stock of their equipment. They'd supplemented their own gear with whatever they'd been able to scavenge from their fallen colleagues, I noted, and were now refilling magazines and reorganising their packs.

"Am I to understand your boss changed his mind?" MacLeod asked, his tone mild.

The sergeant slapped the magazine he'd just loaded against his free hand to seat the rounds, tucked it into a leg pocket and straightened, meeting MacLeod's gaze flat and level. "Well, it would certainly seem that way, wouldn't it?"

The silence stretched between them until at last MacLeod let his breath out in something close to a huff and said, "OK then, what can we do to help?"

It was only then, after the decision was made and they'd seen the way the cards had fallen, that I realised what a knife-edge we'd been balanced on.

I blinked, and the scene was suddenly different. The weapons that had seemed so casually rested were now carefully located that bit closer to each man's hand than I'd noticed before. All the men were crouched rather than sitting, so they were ready to move in an instant if it went against them.

The sergeant's shoulders dropped a fraction and the tension eased out of the rest of his team. His eyes flicked to mine and narrowed slightly. He knew what I'd seen, I realised, and didn't like it much. Maybe he thought they'd been trained to be more subtle than that.

What was it that drove them, I wondered, to be so focused, so intent, that they were prepared to go against their own side to accomplish their goal?

"We're going to need to borrow a couple of your lads—the fittest you've got. Preferably your medic, if you can spare him, and anyone who speaks Pashto or Dari."

I felt my heart stutter a little. I wasn't a medic, and I didn't speak either of the main Afghan languages beyond the usual *hello, how are you? thank you, goodbye.* No chances for me there. Was I disappointed, or relieved?

MacLeod hesitated. "This op—?"

"I can't tell you, sir. I'm sure you appreciate that."

"I wasn't going to ask. What I *was* going to ask was—since these lads are under my command and in my care—is it as high-risk as your boss seemed to suggest?"

The sergeant gave him a grim smile. "More, if anything. More important, too, otherwise we wouldn't be standing on for it. We have a small window of opportunity. Lot to lose. Lot to gain."

"Even after the cost so far?"

"Yes." No hesitation.

"Then tell them as much as you can and I'll offer them the chance to volunteer," MacLeod said. "With no comebacks if they say no. Good enough?"

The sergeant looked like he'd say more but then he just nodded. "Good enough."

6

"It's a shit deal I'm offering," the sergeant said, "but it is what it is." He glanced at the others, who stood spread behind him. There was no fidgeting. Only their eyes tracked constantly and were never still.

I'd listened like an outsider as he made his case with no frills, no obvious exaggerations or evasions. He gave them the bare bones, stark and clear. It was a risky but vital op, and regardless of volunteers or the lack of them, he and the three other Special Forces lads were going on with the job. Take it or leave it.

I watched the effect his words had on the rest of the patrol, as their meaning and the possible repercussions penetrated.

Corporal Brookes needed telling least of all. He'd been tasked with mopping up operations gone bad in the field often enough that he didn't need it spelled out for him. And besides, he'd just had one of the men he'd be replacing die under his care.

He shrugged, apparently blasé, but I saw the muscles work in his throat before he said quietly, "OK, I'm in."

The sergeant nodded to him without speaking. It said more than words.

Across from me, Tate shifted restlessly. He spoke enough Dari to get by, but his Pashto was good—far better than any of the rest of us.

He gave a big sigh. "OK, yeah, fuck it. Why not?"

The sergeant nodded, rolled his shoulders like the two of them had just lifted a weight off him.

"Thank you," he said, like he meant it. "Savour that, lads, because it's the last kind word I'm going to give you until this is all over. Before then, I'll push all of us until you'll wish you'd never joined this man's army, let alone stuck your neck out for it."

"Christ, don't oversell it, whatever you do," Tate muttered.

"Anything else?" Captain MacLeod asked. The sergeant looked up, met the eyes of one of his men and gave a slight shake of his head. The other man glared at him. I could almost hear the silent argument going on between them. What was it they also needed, I wondered, that he was so reluctant to ask for?

The other man was as tall as the sergeant, but bigger all round —his combat jacket sleeves fit tight around his bulging biceps. He was the only one of the group entirely clean-shaven, and looked like he spent most of his down-time pumping iron.

He continued to glare and eventually the sergeant seemed to give in. Without much hope in his voice he asked, "Who's your best shot? Not just *good,* I mean, is anybody outstanding? I'm talking sniper level."

I felt my breath catch in my chest, clog in my throat. My eyes darted to the captain's, but he wouldn't meet my gaze.

MacLeod shook his head, still avoiding eye contact with me. "No way," he said shortly. "Nothing doing there, I'm sorry."

The sergeant's eyebrows had risen sharply. "What happened to putting the choice to the lad in question and letting him decide for himself?"

"Because it's not a 'lad' at all," MacLeod said, ducking his head in my direction. "It's Charlie."

There was a long pause after that. The information wasn't news to any of my own patrol, but they held their breath anyway while they waited to see what the Special Forces team would do next. If they were hoping for something dramatic, they were disappointed. These boys kept everything under control, even their professional disbelief. For the most part, anyway.

The man with the muscles gave a grunt. "OK, so who's *second* best?"

The sergeant silenced him with a brief look, and persisted. "Put it this way, who made the shot that took out the pick-up full of Talis?"

It was Corporal Brookes who answered. "Yeah, that would be Charlie," he said dryly. "Moving target at best part of a thousand metres. Still want our *second* best shot, eh?"

I shifted uncomfortably, aware of every eye on me. "Don't exaggerate, corp. It wasn't anywhere near a thousand metres," I muttered. "It was more like seven hundred."

The sergeant raised one eyebrow, just a fraction. "But you took out the truck rather than the driver," he said. "Luck or intent?"

"How do you know what I hit?" I demanded, stung by the tone of his voice as much as the question.

"Because we had eyes on the target ourselves."

"So why didn't *you* take out the driver, if that was the better option?"

"We were too far out," he admitted. I played back the time to the team appearing at the crash site, and worked out they couldn't have been much further away than I was.

"And I'm not saying what you did wasn't the right choice. Just want to know why you made it."

I let my breath out fast down my nose, tried to keep my voice calm and level. "Because if I'd just shot the driver, what was to stop one of the others kicking him out and taking over the wheel himself? Shoot the driver and lose one enemy gun. But shoot the truck and lose all of them."

And if I was retro-fitting the reasoning to the action, I hoped the conviction I injected into my voice now would obscure it. I looked at the sergeant's unsmiling face and couldn't say for certain if he was taken in by my bravado. Probably not.

"So, the real question is, Charlie, if I told you we were hoping to make use of the pick-up as transport, and that shooting the driver would allow us to do that, would you have the balls to pull the trigger?"

I didn't respond immediately. In truth, I didn't know for sure. I'd been in firefights, sure, but that was a far more visceral experience. Somebody fired at you and you fired back. Not to do so would be suicidal. I'd had targets in my sights and watched them fall, but they had always been trying their best to kill me or my fellow squaddies at the time. In truth, I couldn't say if I'd been the one to drop them or if it was somebody else. And they had never been so far away it qualified as assassination.

Eventually, aware of all eyes on me, I shrugged. "Well, we'll just have to burn that bridge when we come to it, won't we?"

The sergeant gave me a shrug of his own by way of reply, but the man with the muscles made a sound in the back of his throat that might have been a growl.

"Oh, come on—"

The sergeant silenced him with a look more effective than any punch.

"What—you'd rather she gave me some bullshit answer and then cried off?"

The searing look flicked in his direction told me the man with the muscles thought I'd likely cry off anyway, regardless of whatever answer I gave.

"It's a moot point," MacLeod said, his voice hard. "She's not going."

"Thought you were going to give everyone a chance to make up their own minds," the sergeant said. And if the question was for MacLeod, his eyes were on me.

"Yes, but—"

"But what? The army's equal opportunity now, hadn't you heard?" His voice was quiet, dangerously close to jeering. "Every parent has the right to bury a daughter, not just a son."

MacLeod opened his mouth to protest, then shut it again, gave a gesture that was half exasperation and half defeat.

"OK, Charlie—up to you. Nobody can order you into combat, but if you choose to go, well..."

He was frowning as he let the words trail away. As if I was about to disappoint him. As if I was about to make the wrong decision, and by doing so prove that I wasn't ready for this—that I wasn't suitable and never would be.

That came as a shock after all his apparent open-mindedness over my role. The realisation slid down my spine in a cold slither, that lumping me in with the rest of the "lads" was a form of avoidance rather than acceptance.

And if I was still wavering, his next words took away the last shreds of my uncertainty.

"You might want to bear in mind, though, what the Tali are likely to do to you if you're captured."

"I shouldn't imagine what they're likely to do to any of us would be much fun, sir," I said, and it wasn't merely bluster. At that age—at that time—you tend to think you're invincible. I did, that's for sure.

I looked at the three guys behind their sergeant, saw them as individuals for the first time. Big, dark, his face outlined by a scruff of beard growth, the man with the muscles gave off an air of utter confidence in the ability of his own body to drive him forward, no matter what, to overpower and overcome.

The other two I had yet to hear speak. One was small, tight and compact, with the pale translucent skin of the natural redhead, a spray of freckles visible above the cam cream smeared across his face, and pale lashes framing pale eyes.

And the last, taller, slimmer, with an arrogance to his stance, head back so he was using a long nose as a gun sight, aiming right at me, unnerving. I kept my eyes on the sergeant. Not the easy option, by any means. There was something about him that made me wary to the tips of my fingers, and I had a feeling he knew it.

"Is that the kind of thing you need me to do?" I hedged. "Take out the driver of a truck, I mean."

He gave another shrug. "Won't know for sure until it happens. We need someone for overview rather than close-quarter, if that makes you feel any better about it. Someone to watch our backs. But as and when anything *does* kick off, you can't hesitate. If you're going to bottle it, you're no use to us."

The man with the muscles scowled. "We don't have time for this!"

"Not every soldier has the stomach to be a sniper, Charlie, no matter how good a shot they are," MacLeod put in. "No shame in admitting that."

The relief his words engendered was followed by a flick-switch of guilt and then rage. If I was a guy, would my captain be giving me such an easy get-out, or would he be willing me to man up, step up, be worthy of the uniform?

Before I'd absorbed that brief wave of emotions, the arrogant one rocked back on his heels, head tilted, and said in a surprisingly well-brought-up drawl, "OK, so let me just ask you one last question—a tie-breaker, you might call it. I don't suppose by any chance you know how to ride a horse?"

"A horse?" I repeated blankly.

"Yes, you know—big quadruped. Dangerous at both ends and uncomfortable in the middle, as Oscar Wilde would have it."

"I know what one is, but…don't tell me you're going to *ride* into battle?"

He was still looking down his nose at me, but I thought I detected the hint of amusement in those dry tones. "Well, since some *idiot* shot up the truck we were planning to hijack, what other option do we have?"

7

WHEN THE TALIBAN who'd attacked the downed Lynx fled there were fewer of them than when they arrived. Seemingly convinced by Captain MacLeod's pretence of a larger opposing force, they'd left in something of a hurry. No other reason for them to leave valuable assets behind.

Those assets were eight Afghan horses.

They were short, narrow, and shaggy coated. More overgrown pony than horse, with slender legs that looked nowhere near robust enough to handle the ferocious terrain, and cracked, unshod hooves. Their bridles were of leather so brittle it was like cardboard, decorated with intricately beaded straps and tassels. The saddles were little more than wooden boards, padded away from the horses' backs with woven blankets, and covered in goatskins. I was a little alarmed that the stirrup irons seemed barely large enough for the toe of my boot. The leather straps from which they dangled weren't even adjustable. It was a one-size-fits-none deal.

"How do we know this lot aren't booby-trapped?" Tate demanded, eyeing them suspiciously. "How do we know they didn't leave them on purpose, like?"

I glanced at him. "Booby-trapped *how*, exactly?"

"I dunno. They could all be wild. They might throw us off and trample us to death or something."

The well-spoken soldier snorted. "In my experience, you don't actually *have* to booby-trap a horse to get it to do that."

"Again, stop with the overselling, will you?" Tate muttered.

"You've never ridden, have you?"

Tate shifted awkwardly. "'Course I have. Just not horses, eh? But how hard can it be?"

I didn't answer. He'd find out soon enough.

By the carriage of their tails and the slightly dished faces, there was Arab in the horses' breeding somewhere. I could imagine they'd be hardy, quick, but take no prisoners. They were nervy as strangers approached, scuttling to the extent of their tethers, head-shy when I lifted a hand to stroke a flinching shoulder.

The horses had been tethered to whatever was handy, their reins wrapped around rocks, or knotted onto the stubby shrubs. A couple of them had been tied to the saddle of another, the equine equivalent of double parking.

"They brought extra with them," said a voice alongside me in the gloom, making me start. I jerked round to find the sergeant standing less than three paces away, although I could barely see his face. "It wasn't just an ambush—they were hoping for prisoners to carry away with them."

"Does that mean…?" I hesitated. It wasn't my place to speak, wasn't my question to ask.

"Spit it out, soldier."

"Does that mean they knew you were coming?" I blurted in a rush. "Or were they intending to grab the next helo crew who happened by, regardless?"

Helmand province was somewhere close to sixty thousand square kilometres by itself. Hell, the UK as a whole was only two hundred and forty thousand. Besides, taking down a modern helicopter with a shoulder-mounted rocket launcher was not impossible, but it wasn't a certainty, either. The chances of this being opportunistic were practically zero, and we both knew it.

He shrugged. "Hope for the best," he said. "Plan for the worst."

"Oh, *that's* comforting. Do they teach you those sayings in the SAS handbook?"

He paused, and for a moment I couldn't tell if he was deciding on a suitably scathing rebuke.

Then he said, "Actually, I think I got that one out of a fortune cookie down our local Chinese takeaway."

I couldn't quite raise a laugh, but I smiled and realised how tense I'd been, that the joke was deliberate. I tried to see the sergeant's face more clearly but it was in shadow. He unshouldered a rifle, longer than the assault weapon he carried and thrust it at me. It landed heavy in my hands, bulky and alien, smelling of gun oil and smoke.

"You'll need this. First light you can have half a dozen rounds to zero in."

"Half a dozen?"

"Can't spare any more."

I shrugged. There wasn't much else I could say.

He nodded as if I'd spoken anyway, jerked his head towards the horses.

"If you know what you're about with this lot, get your lads ready to go. We're out of here in ten." And with that he turned and was swallowed up by the darkness.

I watched him go, took a breath and gave the rifle in my hands a proper once-over, or as much as I could in the dim light.

The weapon was a heavily camouflaged L115 sniper rifle. I'd seen them on the ranges in training but never come close to firing one. British built by Accuracy International, it was a manual bolt-action with a five-round box magazine snug in front of the trigger, and sturdy spring-loaded bipod legs at the front of the frame. The end of the barrel sported a sound suppressor. A high-power telescopic sight scope was mounted on the top rail.

I tried the rifle up into my shoulder. Even with its relatively compact layout, the weapon had been chosen for a six-foot-plus squaddie in mind and it was far too big for me. If I seated the butt properly, I could barely reach the pistol grip, never mind get my forefinger to the trigger. God knows what would happen when I tried actually firing it.

Ah well, I'll worry about that at first light.

I glanced over and found Captain MacLeod watching me. Not that I could see his face clearly, but I could tell from the angle of his body. He turned away with what might have been a slight shake of his head. The heat was back in my face again as I tried to work out how I went from being a reliable member of his team to a disappointment, so fast.

I slung the rifle over my left shoulder on its strap. It should have balanced up my personal weapon, but all it did was pull me down further. Ignoring the drag on my back, I moved forward, unknotted the reins of a dirty grey horse and led him out of the lines. He didn't want to be parted from his herd-mates, but once the first reluctant side-step was taken, he followed me docilely.

"All yours," I said to Tate, checking the girth-strap was tight enough to hold the saddle on top before handing him over. A couple of our patrol held onto the horse's bridle for him to hoist himself on board, so I left them to it.

I picked out a dark bay mare for Brookes, and a little chestnut with a white face for myself.

"Hey, that's not on! You've gone for the smallest one," Tate protested. "That'll be dead easy to get on and off."

"Yeah, but I weigh less than you do. No point in making the poor little bugger's legs buckle."

"You saying I'm fat?"

"Depends when you last saw your cock without the aid of a mirror, mate," Brookes said cheerfully, getting an upraised middle finger in response.

He was as much of a novice as Tate, but less inclined to bullshit about it. They both looked totally out of sync with the motion of the animal beneath them. You had to anticipate how the horse was going to move and flow with it, not hold yourself so rigid you lurched awkwardly in the saddle every time they took a step.

It seemed the lads assumed I didn't need any help. By the time I came to mount up, they were all conspicuous by their absence. Without anyone to hold the chestnut, he danced about while I hopped in pursuit trying to get onto him. Eventually I gave up stretching for the tiny stirrup, slung the rifle over the front of the saddle, grabbed hold of the pommel and made a jump for it. Undignified, but effective.

I soon found that the wooden boards on his back were just as uncomfortable as they'd looked. Although he'd been skittish on the ground, once I was on top the chestnut didn't seem bothered about what I was doing. He stood without twitching while I wriggled my combat jacket off my shoulders, then stripped out the sleeveless liner and stuffed it underneath me. The night was bitter, but it was a while since I'd ridden and I reckoned bleeding saddle sores would be worse than the cold.

I patted his scrawny neck, silently named him Mones in lieu of anything better. I'd been told it meant 'companion' or 'friend' in Pashto.

"Salaam Alaikum, Mones," I murmured. *Peace be upon you.*

The chestnut flicked back one ear in response.

Meanwhile, the four unmarked soldiers had hauled themselves aboard their own mounts. Only the tall one with the upper-class voice looked as if he'd been anywhere near a horse before. The other three were clearly uncomfortable in the saddle to one degree or another.

Perhaps the sergeant was hiding his unease best. Maybe he'd realised that tensing up was going to make things worse so he sat slumped in the saddle, reins held casually in his left hand. Only the tightness of his grip gave him away.

His assault weapon was in his right, balanced with the butt on his hip. The horse, I assumed, was so accustomed to the sound of close-proximity gunfire it wasn't likely to do anything stupid if he shot from the back of it.

"We set?" he asked. He probably couldn't see the nods he got in reply, but it was a rhetorical question anyway. We were going regardless.

"What about her?" I asked, nodding to the last horse. A grey mare, she was still tied to a spiky bush and was stamping her front hooves in the dusty earth as if to say, "Hey, don't leave me here!" I could see white around the liquid darkness of her eyes and hear her snorts of distress. Horses are herd animals, after all.

"We'll take it," the tall soldier drawled. "Never a bad idea to carry a spare."

One of the lads, Baz, untied the horse and tugged it over towards him, but the tall soldier shook his head.

"I didn't mean *I* would be carrying it personally," he said. He nodded in my direction. "I think you'll find Charlie has a hand free, and aren't women always telling us blokes how good they are at multitasking?"

I tied off the reins to my saddle without comment. There wasn't much I could say that wouldn't have got me into trouble.

Captain MacLeod stepped forward.

"Good luck. And take care of my lads."

"I'll do my best," the sergeant said, "but no promises."

8

Everybody had their quirks when it came to firing a long gun at a target more than a hundred metres away. The greater the distance, the more magnified the quirk.

Mine was a tendency to pull the shot high and right. Especially if I was under observation, under pressure, or thinking about what I was doing too damn much. Needless to say, the first time I fired the L115 sniper's rifle the sergeant had dumped on me, I barely hit the target.

Strangely enough, the Special Forces team made no comment about this poor performance. It was left to Tate, lying alongside and spotting for me, to mutter, "Oh come *on*, Charlie. You're making us all look bad."

I blocked him out, reached up for one of the turret adjustment knobs on the Schmidt and Bender scope, then hesitated, glanced back over my shoulder.

"Are you sure whoever owns this doesn't mind me messing with the settings on his weapon?"

"It's your weapon now, soldier," the sergeant said. "Just do whatever you need to."

I squirmed a little in the dirt, but however I positioned myself, the stock was too big for me. No getting around that.

After a moment or two's useless fidgeting, the sergeant nudged my shoulder. When I looked up, he shooed me away from the gun. I scrambled up, backed away feeling humiliated as he picked the rifle off its bipod legs. One shot had proven my worthlessness, and now I was a spare part. Useless to the team, redundant.

"Hey, where are you going? Come here if you want me to get the damn thing to fit you better. It's like watching my kid brother trying to ride our dad's old bike."

He quickly removed the thick shoulder pad and taped a wadded-up mesh scarf in place over the end of the stock. It wasn't perfect, but at least it was a lot closer to being the right size.

This time when I lay down behind the gun, I didn't feel it was trying to push my arm in totally the wrong direction. I settled myself, slowed my breathing, and aimed for the same blotch on the goatskin they'd strung out six hundred metres away. The suppressor on the end of the barrel reduced the sound to little more than a dull slap.

"That's more like it!" Tate said. "The round landed at two o'clock, about a hundred and fifty mil out from centre."

I ignored the ache in my shoulder. And this time, I didn't ask permission before I adjusted the sight and fired again.

"A hundred mil out, now dead-on twelve o'clock."

I wound the elevation knob a couple of clicks, bringing the crosshairs and the site of my last shot together, then fired a fourth time. That got me closer still. Another adjustment, another shot.

"Bull's-eye! Nice one, mate."

I unclipped the empty five-round magazine and picked up the final practice round the sergeant had allowed me, but hesitated before feeding it in. Instead, I clambered to my feet again, limp with the effort, and passed the round back to the sergeant, resisting the urge to rub my right shoulder where the makeshift pad had recoiled into it. The scarf was no substitute for high density shock-absorbent foam.

"What's this for?"

"You said I had half a dozen to get my eye in. I only needed five."

He considered for a moment, then handed the round back to

me, his expression guarded. "I'd have been more impressed if you'd just put that through the same hole as the last."

Well, that's me told.

We had stopped as the sun hit the tops of the mountains, started to bleed down into the valley we were riding through, turning the dust a golden red. Everyone had dismounted and was walking stiffly, something that only started to dissipate the more we moved around.

Now, Tate went to retrieve my goatskin target six hundred metres down range. Brookes strolled across. "Nice shooting, Charlie."

"Eventually. I just hope I don't mess it up when the time comes."

"Ah, don't sweat it. You'll be fine."

I rolled my eyes. "Such faith—or is that you with your medical head on, looking out for my mental health?"

"Bit of both." He grinned. "Speaking of mental health, how's your arse?"

The segue took me by surprise. "My...what?"

"Sorry, I keep forgetting that unlike most of the lads that's not where you keep your brain. Saddle sores—got any I ought to know about?"

"My arse is fine, thank you," I said primly, "and very much my own."

He laughed. "You know I'll always watch it for you."

"Thanks... I think."

I finished strapping the rifle to the saddle of the little chestnut. Across from me, the sergeant was scanning the surrounding terrain. He'd sent the small red-headed guy and the one with the muscles on ahead when the rest of us stopped so I could zero the gun.

"I've just worked it out who they are," Brookes said suddenly in my ear.

It took my mind a moment to backtrack and realise I had no idea what he was on about. "Who?"

"This lot." He jerked his head towards the sergeant and the taller soldier with the upper-class accent.

I turned, saw his lips twitching. "Go on."

"The Spice Girls!" he said, breaking into a grin. "That's Scary and Posh over there, and the other two are Ginger and Sporty. Wondered why they haven't put out a new single for a bit? Well, it's because they're over here in 'Stan, doing their bit for Queen and country."

I spluttered with laughter. "My God…I think I'll let *you* break it to them that you've uncovered their secret."

"Well, if they're not prepared to tell us their real names, they'll just have to take what they get, won't they?"

———

WE MOUNTED up and moved off soon afterwards, Tate groaning that his arse was getting to the stage where he was even tempted to let Brookes take a look at it.

"Don't need to look at it to know what you need," Brookes said easily. "Got some liniment you can rub into it, if it's bad. Just make sure you wash your hands before you take a leak."

Tate twisted in his saddle and gave me a leer. "Maybe I can get Charlie to rub it in for me, eh?"

"I'm not getting close to *your* arse without a gasmask," I told him. "It's bad enough being able to *hear* it from the other side of camp."

The sergeant—Scary—was riding just ahead of us. Suddenly, he wheeled the dark bay he'd chosen and came back. He turned again alongside Tate so they almost bumped knees, and loomed over to him. The nickname Brookes had come up with had never seemed so apt.

"All right, knock it off," he said with quiet force. "Right now."

"What?" Tate seemed genuinely taken aback. "What the fuck did I do?"

"You got the hots for her, or you two got something going on, I don't care. Just as long as the pair of you keep it in your pants 'til this is over, you hear me?"

Tate's face, already reddened from a combination of both sunburn and windburn, flushed darker still. "I'm not! I mean, there isn't…I—"

"Well leave out the smartarse comments then, sunshine. If they're not true they reflect badly on you."

"And if they are?" I knew it was sheer bravado made Tate ask the question.

The sergeant's eyes swept over me, and just before he wheeled his horse away he said, "Then they reflect badly on her."

9

My first few return visits after undergoing basic training did not enamour me to my parents any more than joining up had done to begin with.

But the third—or was it the fourth?—hit a new low. It had nothing to do with coming home in uniform, because as ever I was in civvies. It had everything to do with the way I arrived there.

On a motorcycle.

The old Yamaha RD350 LC was the first bike I bought that didn't come with Learner plates as standard. I'd passed my motorcycle test and the open road, including all the motorways of England, was my playground. I intended to make the most of it.

I hadn't told my parents I was taking lessons, never mind that I'd got my licence and bought the Yam. Well, if you know they're going to be pissed off, why not get it all out of the way at once?

It was a nice theory.

Even as I pulled up—still a little gingerly, I admit—on the expanse of loose gravel in front of the house, I caught sight of my mother's figure at one of the tall drawing room windows. It didn't take much imagination to paint a frown on her face at the arrival of some apparent hooligan.

I wasn't the only visitor, I saw. There was a two-year-old

Range Rover pulled up by the front door. It had 'county set' written all over it. But I was willing to bet the thumping great 4x4 had never seen a splash of mud up the sides of its gleaming bodywork, and the nearest it ever got to actually being off road was parking on a grass verge.

By the time I'd killed the engine and toed down the bike's side stand, my mother was hovering in the open doorway, fingers of one hand playing anxiously with the strand of pearls at her throat. I tugged the strap of my helmet loose and peeled it off, revealing reddened cheeks imprinted with the weave of the lining, and a very bad case of sweaty hat-hair.

"Charlotte! I–I didn't know you were coming, darling," she said, her voice pitched too high. She swallowed and brought it down to a level where passing bats were not endangered, stepping out onto the drive. "Aren't you supposed to be on your…course?"

The reason for her prevarication became clear when two other women appeared behind her from the hallway, not quite goggling at me, but not far off. I vaguely recognised the older woman. I didn't know her name but I knew the type well enough. Some crony of my mother's from the paramilitary fundraising wing of the local Women's Institute.

She moved past with a gracious smile, followed by a younger carbon copy who could only be her daughter or her clone. There was a uniformity of style to their outfits that showed less variation than army kit. I was the only one not wearing pearls.

"It's been *so* lovely to see you, Elizabeth," the woman said. She air-kissed my mother's cheek while eyeing me at the same time over her shoulder.

"Oh yes, absolutely," the daughter wittered. "Thanks awfully for afternoon tea. It was simply lovely. You *must* give me the recipe for that delicious cake."

"Yes, lovely," my mother murmured vaguely.

The woman blipped the Range Rover's locks and hurried towards it as if afraid I might be contagious. "Come along, Diana."

I rested my lid on the Yamaha's tank and regarded the pair of them. I knew the daughter, I realised. We'd competed against each other in Pony Club gymkhanas only a few years previously. Now it seemed decades ago.

We must have been about the same age but there the similarity ended. She wore a pleated wool skirt and twinset in a dirty pink shade that was probably called 'heather'. I wasn't sure if it made her look prematurely middle-aged, or like a six-year-old playing dress-up in mummy's clothes.

"Hello, Charlotte," she said, slightly breathless at daring to defy her mother's summons. "Gosh, that's never *your* motorbike! Surely you don't *ride* that, do you?"

I paused a beat. What did she think I did—took it in a taxi? "Yes, it is," I said. And when the devil on my shoulder prodded me with his pitchfork, I added, "Why, want to take it for a spin?"

She laughed and shook her head, and just for a moment I thought I spotted something regretful in her face. I remembered then that the pony Diana used to ride back when I'd known her was a lunatic who carted her off into the distance on a regular basis, and was prepared to jump or barge through any obstacle in its path. I'd admired her guts. Now, as her mother practically dragged her into the Range Rover and they disappeared down the drive, it seemed she rather admired mine.

"Oh, *Charlotte*," my mother protested, still waving to the departing 4x4. I waited to see if she was going to elaborate but that seemed to be the sum total of her indignation. I knew I'd embarrassed her in front of a woman who, while unlikely to be a friend, was certainly one of her social peers. No, I decided, she had simply just compared me to Diana and found me wanting in every way, from dress to attitude. She sighed. "I wish you'd let me know you were coming, darling."

I shrugged as I swung my leg over the back of the bike to dismount, stiff after the long journey. "Didn't know for certain I was coming until this morning," I fibbed. "I'm about to be posted. They've been cancelling leave on us left, right and centre."

"Oh…well, do come on in, then. I'll make a fresh pot of tea. And I'm sure your father will be…pleased to see you."

She turned away as she spoke, but not before I caught the

flash of something in her eyes. If I didn't know her better, it might almost have been fear.

'PLEASED' was not exactly the word I would have used to describe my father's reaction to my presence—or to that of the Yamaha.

He actually came out of his study to inspect my mode of transport, sniffing as he registered its age, engine size, and mileage. All of which were higher numbers than suited him.

He wore dark green moleskin trousers and a Tattersall check shirt under a jumper that was probably cashmere.

"If your mother and I had known you were thinking of buying a vehicle, Charlotte," he said at last, "I'm sure we could have contributed towards a little car of some sort."

"I didn't want a car," I said, trying not to grind the enamel off my teeth. "I'm happy with the bike, thanks."

He made a noncommittal kind of grunt and led the way back inside. In his study he pulled out several manila folders from his filing cabinet and handed them to me. I opened the top one with cautious curiosity, skimmed the first couple of short paragraphs before glancing up in surprise.

"Are these case notes from your patients?"

He regained his chair behind the desk and steepled his fingers before nodding. "Redacted, of course. I'm writing a paper for the Journal," he said. "On surgical techniques to repair injuries sustained in motorcycle accidents."

Anger manifested as a sudden heat in my face, a coldness in my hands. "I know the risks, and I'm careful."

He didn't try to argue or dissuade me. "The only thing I ask is that you ride with the correct protective clothing," he finished, gesturing to my ordinary denim jeans and trainers. I might almost have thought he cared, until he added, "It makes reconstructive work so much easier."

"I have a leather jacket and decent gloves."

"But not protective legwear or the proper boots," he pointed out. "In my experience, by far the largest percentage of injuries sustained in motorcycle accidents are to the legs and feet—up to and including amputation."

I grimaced and dropped the file back onto his desk. "Yeah, thanks for that."

"If it's a matter of money—"

"No, it isn't," I cut in. "But I'm touched by the offer."

For a moment the silence stretched and tore between us. He cleared his throat. "How is your military training going?"

"Why? Are you going to offer to buy me better body armour for that as well?"

He stared at me over the top of his reading glasses, just long enough for me to feel small.

"Good. It's good." I huffed out a breath. "I just took my APWT and scored high enough to qualify for Marksman."

"APWT?"

"Annual Personal Weapon Test."

"Ah, I see." A pause. "And what purpose does being classified as a marksman serve?"

I opened my mouth to snap at him for such a dumb question, then realised I didn't have a prepared answer. We'd already been told that however good a shot we managed to become, as women in this man's army, it was only ever going to serve us well in theory or in competition.

"Well," I said at last, "if they ever *do* decide to allow the odd female soldier to reach the sharp end of the military, it looks like I'll be one of them, then, doesn't it?"

10

WE CAUGHT up with the others—I could now think of them by no names other than Sporty and Ginger—two hours later, above a small collection of patched and crumbling buildings in the bottom of a valley. They were lying out of sight in the rough scrub a little way back from the crest, keeping watch on the comings and goings, and pulled back to meet us when I raised them over the Bowman CNR. We were too far out for the personal radios to operate, particularly in this kind of terrain.

"All quiet," was how Sporty described the village. "No strangers in. No strangers out."

"How can you tell who's a stranger and who isn't?" I asked.

Sporty glanced at me sharply but there was no challenge in my face or tone. It was a simple question.

"For peasants, they can be very formal," he said grudgingly, a moment later. "There are ways of treating guests that's different from family. Trust me, I'd know if any of the people we've seen were outsiders. Nothing doing here."

"So far," Ginger agreed. "Of course, the smart thing would be to keep tabs on them for another day or so, though."

The sergeant, Scary, shook his head. "We don't have that luxury."

He nodded to the Bowman, indicating the message I'd picked up on the way in. It was in code—an apparently meaningless short phrase. I'd given them a read-back and passed it on to the sergeant, who hadn't needed a translation. He told me to answer with a simple "received and understood" in plain language.

Now he said, "The failed attack on the helo put the wind up them."

Sporty made a noise close to a snort. "Define 'failed' for me there, would you?"

"Failed to capture any of us or kill all of us," Scary said without missing a beat. "According to the chatter, the meeting has been brought forward twenty-four hours."

Sporty swore, turning away as if to curtail some worse reaction. Ginger went very still, eyes flicking over the sergeant's face.

"So…what d'you reckon?"

Scary shrugged. "I reckon it's a bad idea, but this whole thing was half arsed to start with, so why should anything change now?" He looked to Brookes. "Here's the thing. One of the chief guy's nephews has been sick for a while. They've asked if our medic can take a look at him. It could be genuine, or it could be a setup, but it's what they want in return for helping us. You up for risking it?"

Brookes blew out a long breath. "How old is he?

"The nephew? About five or six."

Brookes nodded, like that tipped the balance. "Best do it then, eh?"

"OK."

Automatically, I got to my feet, but Scary stopped me with a look. "Not you, Charlie."

Tate grinned. "If these are peasants, they still keep their women barefoot and pregnant and chained to the kitchen sink. Don't want to shock 'em, do we?"

He seemed unfazed by the vicious glares thrown by the sergeant as well as me. They flashed across and thudded in around him like knives in a circus act.

"I was going to say I planned to keep her on the outside as a kind of Get Out of Jail Free card," Scary said mildly. He paused, "But we will need an interpreter, so *you're* coming."

Tate's grin fell away. I was careful not to let one sprawl across my own face in response. You go asking for something and you can't be too surprised when you get it.

Scary glanced across at Ginger and Sporty. "You two stay up here with Charlie."

"Don't tell me—overwatch." Ginger's voice was resigned. "OK, pal. If the worst comes to the worst, we'll do what we can."

It wasn't lost on me that he glanced at Sporty rather than me as he spoke. And in truth I didn't know whether to be insulted or relieved.

I helped Tate and Brookes climb back onto their horses, on the grounds that I may as well act as groom if nothing else. As I tightened the girth strap on the bay mare Brookes was riding, I wished him luck.

"Thanks," he said with a thin smile. "As long as this kid's got something I can a) diagnose and b) treat, then hey, what is there to worry about?"

I patted the mare on her narrow shoulder as he turned her away and nudged his heels into her sides. Not a horseman yet, by any means, but he was picking it up.

The sergeant waited until we had moved forward and set up in what little cover was available before the group started out. They circled to a well-worn path and began to descend towards the village. The horses moved carefully, picking their way down as the incline steepened. Their hooves slid away from under them on the loose scree with unnerving regularity. All I saw was a sudden lurch, then both horse and rider seemed to disappear in a cloud of choking dust. After a beat they'd emerge, the horse snorting and shaking the dirt out of its ears and the rider clinging on for grim death. Not easy to try to look relaxed and unthreatening under the circumstances. I'm not entirely sure they carried it off.

I tracked their progress through the Schmidt and Bender scope, aware of Ginger alongside me and Sporty a little way off to my right. Ginger's eyes were fixed to the scene below.

"And we have movement," he murmured, his tone of voice suggesting it had been only a matter of time.

"Where?"

"You see the bombed-out house? Next to the other bombed-out house."

"Yeah, thanks, that's really not—"

But I caught a glimmer of movement then through my free eye, and realised guiltily I should have been watching the buildings more closely rather than our guys. I hutched my body sideways, pivoting the rifle from the back rather than lift and reposition the front bipod legs, screwing them into the dirt.

"Ah, OK. I have him," I muttered. A skinny figure in a long grey *kameez* shirt that flapped about his knees as he ran, a dark waistcoat with an upright collar, and a rounded skullcap that I vaguely remembered was called a *kufi*. "A kid—teens, maybe."

"Age means nothing. Arse, I've lost him. Can you see him? His hands? What's in his hands?"

"Wait one… Ah, there. No, nothing. Hands are clear."

"I got him. Arms are swinging. Always check that. If he's not moving his arms, chances are he's hiding something under his clothing. Look for arm swing, a natural kinda gait, OK?"

"Have that."

"Jeez, pal, did you go to a posh school or what?"

"What?" I whispered sharply, trying to keep my jaw clamped shut both so my face didn't shift against the stock and so I didn't take in a mouthful of dust. "What does that have to do with anything?"

"Maybe 'cause you don't say 'roger that' like one of us normal folk."

"Oh aye, dead posh, that's me," I muttered back, deliberately squashing my accent flat. "I lift me pinkie finger when I drink me tea an' all."

He gave a soft chuckle and despite everything that was going on I felt a little of the tension ease out of my neck and arms. Which was, I realised, the reason why he'd done it.

"Where's the kid now?"

"Just approaching one of the houses." I checked the shadows, made a swift calculation. "On the northeast side of the main street. One of the few that *doesn't* looked as though it's been bombed."

"The biggest one—with the compound?"

"That's it."

"Watch the roof. If they're planning an ambush, that's the logical place to do it from. They'd have the elevation, with a bit of stonework for cover."

His voice betrayed no emotion at the possibility of two of his fellow team members being waylaid and slaughtered. *And two of* my *team along with them.*

I swallowed past the lump in my throat. "I, em, thought this was Pashtun territory."

"So?"

"Don't they have some kind of ethical code—about offering hospitality to strangers?"

"*Pashtunwali,* aye," Ginger agreed. "But there are some who'd argue that *melmastia,* as they call being friendly to visitors, doesn't apply when you're dealing with infidels and heathens the likes of us."

More people appeared from houses. All men. They carried weapons—old Lee-Enfields and the occasional AK—but mainly slung over their shoulders rather than readied to fire.

They watched the group of horsemen ride sedately into the village, closing in around them and pointing the way to the house where the boy had disappeared. As they reached it and halted, an older man came out. He was dressed in the same loose trousers and long shirt, but immaculate in pale cream. From the way the others deferred to him, I guessed the newcomer was the local chief Scary had mentioned. Alongside him were several younger men, all dressed in similar clothing. All had beards. All were armed.

I forced myself to keep scanning the rooftops while a brief exchange took place in the street. Scary brought Tate up alongside him to translate, and they motioned in Corporal Brookes' direction a couple of times.

Whatever Tate said to him, the chief seemed happy. After a few minutes, all four dismounted and were ushered into the house. Their horses were led away. The men who'd gathered at their arrival dispersed as if under curfew. Before long, the dirt street was eerily empty again. It was as if they had gone into hiding.

11

"What the hell's taking them so long?" I demanded. I hadn't looked at my watch, but it seemed like hours had passed. Sweat glued my combats to my back and I could feel the sharp outline of every rock and pebble on the ground beneath me. My mouth was so dry I could hardly work up a spit.

Ginger threw me a sideways glance, although he had a rivulet of sweat running down the side of his face.

"Patience, eh? Like I said, these people have very set ideas in the way they go about things. You can't rush 'em if you expect to get anything out of 'em."

"Yeah, but you would have thought, if the chief's nephew is so ill, they might hurry things along a bit."

"Depends how good your corporal is at his job, I guess, doesn't it?"

I still had the sergeant's admonishment in my head about getting too close to any of my comrades for comfort, so I said cautiously, "I'd trust him."

Ginger grunted. "Well, for all we know, he's sorting the kid out as we speak then, eh?"

"Hm. That doesn't mean I have to like how long it's taking, though."

"Aye, well, can't say I like it much, either."

"Hey. If you two have finished bitching and moaning," Sporty cut in over his PRR, "it looks like we've got company."

"Where?" Ginger squirmed on his belly.

"Southeast. That dust is either being kicked up by horses, or the Afghanis have acquired a shitload of cattle from somewhere, and they're stampeding."

I started to shift, too, but Ginger grabbed my arm before I'd done more than catch the briefest glimpse of the approaching dust cloud.

"Stay on target," he snapped. "Your job is to cover the team."

I swung my sights back to the rooftop, and felt immediate guilt at having to report: "I've got movement on the roof."

"Be specific!"

"One guy. Local dress. Armed with an AK, but doesn't look like he's prepping to defend from attack—he's too relaxed. Now he's waving his arms. Signalling, maybe?"

Ginger swore under his breath. He clicked the pressel of his PRR. "Team Bravo, Team Bravo. Sit-rep needed, over."

"Team Echo," Scary's voice acknowledged over the short-range net. "Wait one, over."

"Team Bravo. Sorry mate, but *urgent* sit-rep needed, over."

The sergeant didn't question that urgency. Instead, after a moment's pause he simply asked, "Approximate ETA?"

"Approaching at speed. As yet no visual confirmation."

"OK, keep us posted."

"How's the kid?"

"Brookes reckons it looks like scarlet fever and is putting an IV line into the boy to rehydrate him. He's been sick for long enough to make it serious."

"Well, tell him to get a shift on, will you? And can you find out if the chief's expecting more visitors?"

"Will do. Wait one," Scary said again, and the net went quiet.

Meanwhile, the approaching dust cloud had thickened. It had gained the soundtrack of pounding hoof beats and shouting men that carried on the still air. The man I'd spotted on the rooftop was joined by a second, both of them staring keenly in the direction of the advancing men. The pair looked more excited than worried by the imminent new arrivals.

As the group reached the outskirts of the village, there had still been no word from Team Bravo on the chief's reaction. Ginger tried raising them again. No response.

"Team Bravo, Team Bravo, please acknowledge my last transmission, over."

Silence.

I flicked my aim away from the rooftop, down into the dirt street outside the house. The horsemen poured into the space, filling it with shaggy mounts that skittered and shied. The men were all armed, dressed in the same mixture of loose *shalwar kameez* clothing as the villagers, which made it hard to identify who was who, or where their allegiances might lie. I risked voicing the question to Ginger.

"Who knows. If we're lucky, they're another local tribe—one who's prepared to help us."

"And if we're not?"

"Then they're fuckin' Tali."

My body temperature went from overheated to freezing in less than the time it took him to say it. I gave a shiver, hairs suddenly upright on my exposed forearms. I'd been in firefights with insurgents before, of course I had. No way to avoid it during my tour to date. But I'd never been in the position of knowing a team of friendlies was in imminent danger of abduction, with all the resultant horrors, and felt so helpless to do anything about it.

"Team Bravo—"

This time it was Sporty who interrupted him. "Hey. Main door, ground level. They're coming out."

Sure enough, I saw Brookes appear in the doorway. He faltered a little when he saw the horsemen milling in the street, and then lurched as he was thrust from behind. Tate stumbled out after him, as if he'd shoved and been shoved in his turn.

Scary and Posh followed them. The two Special Forces guys didn't look more relaxed than the other two, exactly, but possibly less tense. Or they were better at hiding it. All of them had been relieved of their comms and weapons. The village men who'd been part of the welcome committee were now surrounding them, guns levelled. The smiles had disappeared.

I murmured, "Ah...shit."

"Switch to the alternate frequency," Ginger ordered. As I complied I felt rather than saw his gaze swing to me. "Do you have a clear shot?"

I'd curled my finger inside the trigger guard almost on a reflex before the meaning of the question hit. I swallowed. "On who?"

"On the chief."

"Whoa! Hold off on that, mate," Sporty protested. "No telling what these mad bastards will do if we take out their boss man."

Anxiety warred with relief, a whole tumble of emotions that bounced off each other as they rolled around inside. Besides, visible centred in the crosshairs of my scope, the chief himself looked unsettled by events, if not quite full-on angry. I got the impression he was just as surprised by what was happening, but was simply hiding it better.

I noticed he glanced at one of the younger men several times, and although his crinkled face bore no expression, I sensed censure coming off him in waves. I recognised the focus of his disapproval as one of the two men who'd been on the roof. The ones who'd waved to the approaching force with such enthusiasm. A picture, they say, is worth a thousand words. Well, certainly a few hundred rounds in this case.

In the street below us, the four members of Team Bravo stood motionless as the new group of riders jostled around them. One of the riders got too close and his horse swung its hindquarters into Posh—by accident or design, I couldn't tell. He simply braced his shoulder without budging an inch. The horse darted aside. Even so, I reckoned the show was calculated to intimidate rather than injure...for now, at least.

At some unheard signal, the riders swirled back, smooth as an organised equestrian display team, leaving the four men standing in the centre of a clear circle. I felt my stomach clench. The space around them was suddenly more frightening than when they were being crowded.

One of the riders nudged his horse forward a little in front of them, shouting as he weaved back and forth. He was a short, thickset man who held weapon and reins in one hand, and gestured wildly with the other while he spoke. It was impossible to tell if he was arguing in favour of clemency or execution.

The village chief, I noted, stood quiet and said nothing in their defence. I thought of Scary's last transmission, that Brookes had diagnosed his nephew and begun treatment. What was the point of trying to win over hearts and minds, when you were stabbed in the back in the attempt?

The horses our lads had ridden to the village were led out again, and this seemed to provoke the man doing the talking all the more. His gestures became wilder, his finger stabbing in accusation from horses to men.

"I'm guessing they've recognised one or two of those ponies," Ginger said, "and they can put two and two together about how we got hold of 'em."

Sporty swore under his breath, and when he spoke his voice was bitter. "Like we said before—she should have taken out the pickup driver and left us the truck undamaged."

I swallowed back words in my own defence. Instead, it was Ginger who muttered, "Yeah, 'cause they'd never be likely to recognise their own bloody truck…"

12

When the men we assumed were Taliban forces left the village, taking the four prisoners with them, Sporty, Ginger and I were not far behind.

It wasn't hard to track them when their horses kicked up a trail in the dirt we could have followed in the dark. Even so, we kept far enough back that we hoped our presence would pass unnoticed. It was a fine balance between not losing them, and not getting ourselves caught in the process.

My first thought had been to get on the Bowman and call in air support—any kind of support—to try to get our guys back. Ginger and Sporty's response to that suggestion was a short, sharp negative. No time, for one thing, not to mention that they didn't have much faith in the ability of the helo gunship jockeys not to kill friend along with foe. The unspoken reason, I gathered, was that it was their own mess and they wanted to be the ones to clean it up.

The Taliban loaded our guys back onto their horses, wrists tied and reins firmly in the hands of another rider. Disarmed and heavily outnumbered, there wasn't much they could do but, literally, sit tight and go along for the ride. Even so, they'd been roughed up before the journey began, just to knock any bravado out of them.

It had been bloody hard to watch it happen. Doubly difficult when I was doing so through the scope of a sniper's rifle, with the means to bring down instant death on the perpetrators by the slightest squeeze of my right forefinger. Perhaps it was the knowledge of just how easy it would be that stayed my hand. Not to mention that Ginger would have skinned me.

And I knew the retribution that would follow such an action on my part would have been far worse. So I held off, and tried not to let the beatings sicken me. Both Tate and Brookes looked shell-shocked by it all. They'd been warned, but the brutal reality of capture had only just started to truly penetrate. It made what was still to come all the more frightening.

Now, the plan was to get them back before anything worse happened.

Having twenty or so horses churn up the ground before us, there wasn't any necessity to ride single file in an attempt to disguise our number. We rode three abreast where the terrain allowed, keeping our pace down so as not to tire the horses too badly, or risk a fall. We were outnumbered enough, without further depleting manpower through injury.

Ginger rode in the centre, and spent the first twenty minutes or so turned away from me, conversing with Sporty in tones too low to hear.

Eventually, I nudged my horse on ahead and then pulled him sideways in front of the pair, blocking their path and bringing their mounts to a sudden halt.

"OK, enough," I said. "One of you needs to talk to me."

"What's up? You fed up with not being the centre of attention?" Sporty demanded.

I sighed. "Look, I know I'm only a regular squaddie, but I don't have to take my boots and socks off to count to ten, you know."

"I'll take your word on that. So what?"

"So don't treat me like I'm dumb. What's going on?"

They eyed me in silence for a moment, while their horses fidgeted and twitched their ears against the flies.

"You're better off not knowing," Ginger said at last. "Trust me."

"Bollocks to that. Whatever plan you had went sideways as

soon as our lads were taken. If you expect me to play any kind of intelligent role in getting them back, you're going to have to bring me up to speed—on the basics, if nothing else."

The two men exchanged a glance, then Ginger said, "You have to admit she's got a point."

"And if they grab her?" Sporty argued. "She won't last five minutes, mate."

"Maybe not," I agreed. "But how long do you think Tate or Brookes will last when they start roasting their balls over an open fire?"

Ginger raised an eyebrow in silent question to Sporty. Sporty shrugged, which seemed to be an answer in itself.

Ginger blew out a long breath and kicked his horse forward, forcing mine to back off. I twitched my reins and we fell into step alongside.

"OK," he said, "I'm risking the boss ripping me a new one for telling you any of this, but I s'pose you've got a right to know." He paused as if collecting his thoughts. "There was a group of civilian engineers, supposed to be advising on some big electricity generation project further up the Helmand River at the Grishk Dam. The coalition reckon bringing power and irrigation to the farmers will win 'em lots of brownie points with the locals."

"Give her the short version will you, mate?" Sporty said as he manoeuvred his mount onto the other side.

Ginger twisted in his saddle. "For fuck's sake. D'you want to tell it, or what?"

Despite everything, I almost smiled at the matching scowls on their faces. "So, how long *have* you two been married, exactly?"

"Too bloody long," Ginger muttered. "Anyway, to cut a long story short," he added pointedly, "the engineers got themselves kidnapped, held for ransom, but what the Taliban really wanted out of 'em was info on the infrastructure plan."

"What were they doing that's so important?"

Ginger shook his head. "That's above my pay grade, eh—and yours. And it's pretty fuckin' irrelevant, too. What *isn't* irrelevant is that we got word the Al'Qaeda high command have decided to send one of their top interrogators across the border from

Pakistan to torture the engineers for what they know. Guy known as Al-Ghazi—means a warrior who fought for Islam, but we don't think it's his real name. He's a proper sadistic wee fucker, by all accounts."

"So your job was to get in there and spirit the engineers away before Al-Ghazi could get his hands on them?" I guessed.

Ginger flicked me a smile. "Not only that, but to see if we could grab Al-Ghazi himself while we were about it."

"Hm, and how's that working out for you so far?" I asked. "Were you blown, or was the whole thing a setup from the start?"

Ginger grimaced. "Either way, it's been a clusterfuck right from the beginning. No proper planning time, half-arsed intel…" His voice trailed off and he shook his head as if too disgusted to say more.

"To be honest, we probably should have given it up when they hit us on the way in," Sporty admitted. "We don't know for sure if this Al-Ghazi bloke is even going to be there."

"Well let's hope for our lads' sakes that he isn't," Ginger said. "Though, if that's the case, you have to wonder why they bothered taking the prisoners away from the village. Why not just kill 'em right there?"

"Yeah, thanks for putting the thought of something worse in my head," I said sourly. "I hadn't got past being grateful they were still alive."

Ginger gave me a lopsided grin. "Aye, if Al-Ghazi is on his way, your guys are about to face something that will make having their balls roasted seem like a gentle massage with warm towels, eh?"

13

For the second time in twenty-four hours, I found myself lying on hard stony ground, watching a distant tableau that was overlaid by the reticle of a sniper's scope.

The worrying thing was that it was starting to seem normal.

I had a sudden vision of the same overlay but this time the scene was of my parents sitting at the wrought-iron table on the terrace at home. Of centring my sights first on my father's open copy of the *Financial Times* and imagining a small ripped hole appearing in the centre of the front page. Then on the Royal Doulton teapot and watching it shatter in my mother's hands.

I blinked, shook my head and the image faded, to be replaced by an encampment in the Afghan wilderness, a campfire surrounded by misshapen tents. At each side were two stretched out lines, staked in at the ends, to which were tethered their horses.

The sun went down an hour before, dropping like a stone through brief amber into the blue tones of twilight and then darkness. Through the night sights clipped to my day scope, the campfire glowed hot and bright against a ghostly green background. I tried to keep my focus away from the flames so any activity near the tents was more easily visible, but the way they were spread around the camp, it wasn't easy. We needed more eyes on the target.

We needed more of everything.

It didn't help that they'd split the prisoners between two of the tents on differing sides of the camp. The sergeant—Scary—and Tate in one, and Posh and Brookes in another. I'd no idea why they chose those pairings, except perhaps it was obvious who the Special Forces lads were, and they wanted to keep them apart.

"Why couldn't they have put them all in one place?" I muttered, as I tracked yet again across the camp, shutting my eyes briefly past the scorch of the fire.

"Makes sense," Ginger said quietly from alongside me. "Divide and conquer. Less likely to do something stupid if they don't know where their pals are and they might be at risk."

"I'd do the same thing," Sporty admitted. "Put each of 'em on their own if I had enough men to keep an eye on 'em that way."

Half a dozen of the Taliban fighters had ridden out at last light. We didn't have the manpower to follow them, so it wasn't a hard decision to stick with the group holding the prisoners instead. We didn't know how long they'd be gone, or what their purpose was. But it didn't take imagination to work out it wasn't anything good. It made sense that, with the enemy forces depleted, we were never going to get as good or timely an opportunity to mount a rescue.

"So, how are we going to do this?"

"Going to do what?" Ginger queried. "If we attempt to go in there, the chances are they'll have killed the second lot of hostages before we're halfway to freeing the first."

"Can't we go for both at once?"

Sporty let out a snort. "This is not the movies, and though I can understand how you might think so, neither of us is Rambo."

"This kind of op calls for three teams," Ginger said. "Two for the insertion—"

"—and the third for overview," I finished for him. "Yeah, I think I can work that one out."

"Where we're down to two men, never mind two teams," Sporty said.

I lifted my head away from the stock. "Excuse me?"

"OK, two and a half."

"Up yours."

"Knock it off, will you?" Ginger said tightly. "What it means is, we may have to…prioritise."

The sudden dryness in my mouth had little to do with the last time I'd taken a sip of tepid water from the plastic canteen attached to my webbing. "You mean…rescue one lot and not the other?"

"If we have to."

"What are you going to do—toss a bloody coin?"

He sighed. "What choice have we got? Either die trying to get them all out, or fanny around and wait for those bastards to kill them?"

While I was still searching for the voice to answer, Sporty said, "So, who wins tonight's star prize?"

"Ah, fuck. You know that as well as I do, pal."

"You're going to go for your sergeant, aren't you?" I realised.

And Tate, of course. He was a fellow squaddie. Someone I'd sat around with, heard stories about his family, seen pictures of his girlfriend. He was someone I would normally have done my utmost to fight alongside and whose rescue I would have celebrated with the rest.

But if it was a toss-up between him and Brookes… Brookes was closer to being a real friend. There wasn't anything going on between us, but under other circumstances maybe there might have been. Losing him would hit me, and hit me hard. And what about Posh—one of their own team?

"You think it's an easy decision?" Ginger demanded, as if privy to my thoughts. "I wish there was a way around it, but there fucking isn't. And if we sit here with our thumbs up our arses whinging about it, they're all for the chop."

"Surely…" my brain went surging ahead, desperation firing the synapses like the rotary barrels on a GE-Minigun, spitting out thoughts, facts, suggestions. "Surely," I began again, more confidently this time, "if the positions were reversed and they'd grabbed you two instead, what would you be doing in there right now?"

I heard a rustle from Sporty that might have been a shrug in the gloom. "Trying like a man possessed to get loose, I expect," he said. "But they used those plastic zip-ties. They've got a phenomenal breaking strain on 'em. Why d'you think we use 'em ourselves?"

I glanced at his bulging biceps. "Supposing you *did* manage to get free. Then what?"

Another rustle—another shrug. "Wait for an opportunity to make an escape, either evading the guards or grabbing a weapon from one of them. Get to the others if I could. Get the fuck out of there if I couldn't."

"So?" I encouraged.

"So if we go in there the chances are we'll meet them already on the way out," Ginger said, his voice strengthening as the idea took hold.

I nodded. "Then we provide overview, for which—as has been pointed out—you're only two *men* down."

Sporty's head turned towards me and I caught the faint gleam of his teeth in the darkness. "Nah, I think you'll find we're only one-and-a-half men down, mate."

14

I WAS GETTING PRETTY FED up of lying in the dirt. My joints ached from too little activity, and my eyes ached from too much. It was the low hours with dawn still a long way off. The dozy hours, much favoured for raids by police and soldiers alike.

I was still keeping obs on the camp, but now I was alone in the crow-black night. Through the enhanced vision of my scope, I watched the two figures of Ginger and Sporty, moving smooth as liquid over the terrain that separated us from the prisoners' tents.

For all their macho talk, when it came down to it I could see clearly that the guys were shit-hot at what they did. It was hard to remember they were working in the dark. Their movements had the air of free climbers, shifting their weight from one fingertip hold to the next, delicate as a dance, utterly intent on covering the loose ground without stutter or stumble to give them away.

Under other circumstances, it would have been a pleasure to watch.

Now though, the tension had my stomach twisting into knots. Under my fingerless tactical gloves, my palms slid with sweat as the two men skirted the camp, using the tent Scary and Tate were in to shield their approach from the guards.

Perhaps a dozen men had been left on watch. Half of them sat huddled close to the fire, despite the ruinous effect the flames would have on their natural night vision. I guessed from their desultory manner that their leader had gone with the advance party, otherwise discipline would have been tighter. As it was, they talked and spat and drank a spiced tea called *kahwah*, flavoured with cardamom, cinnamon and saffron, and sweetened with honey to the point it made your teeth itch. The smell of it drifted downwind to me on the gentle flutter of breeze. I'd found *kahwah* far too sickly when I'd tried it. Now I longed for a taste.

Because their own view of the guards was blocked by the tent, I was acting as Sporty and Ginger's eyes on scene. Mainly this consisted of issuing stop/go commands whenever any of the guards shifted position, or went to take a piss at the edge of the camp.

It took the two Special Forces men an agonising half hour to cover the distance to the rear of the tent. I saw Ginger crouch by the back wall and ease a combat knife out of its sheath.

"Wait one." I was struggling to keep my voice from emerging as a squawk.

"What?"

Panning rapidly across the camp, I said, "Guards are restless." I shifted further to the right. "Something in the other tent. Go now."

Not without effort, I brought my gaze back across to the first tent, kept it there long enough to see Ginger slit the back wall. The blade sliced through the coarse fabric, clean and quick, like it was silk. He melted inside, leaving Sporty to watch his back.

I panned to the second tent again—the tent where Posh and Brookes were being held—trying to remember to breathe. Two guards were approaching, cautious, AKs in their hands. Their gait was jerky with tension, voices high and harsh. I was close enough to hear them and, not for the first time, wished I understood more than the odd word of it.

When the guards were only a few metres away, the front canvas wall of the tent suddenly billowed outwards as if punched. They both reared back in shock, uttering what could only have been curses, then each checked that the other hadn't clocked the reaction. To admit to fear was to lose face. Bravery in every situation was a cultural necessity for these men. It was their strength and their weakness.

There was a pause like an indrawn breath, then both men opened up. The noise seemed amplified by the darkness, shocking and brutal. With the Kalashnikovs on full auto, each kept the trigger held hard until the magazine was empty and there was nothing left of the second tent but tatters.

15

I DON'T REMEMBER SHOUTING, but the outburst of swearing from Ginger and Sporty over the net told me I must have begun yelling into their earpieces.

The two guards who'd destroyed the tent swung towards my location. The ones who'd been by the fire began to scramble for their own weapons. I rolled sideways moments before the first rounds hit, pinging off stones and kicking up spurts of dust as they sizzled past into the night.

I sprawled into a new position, trying to wedge my elbows in firmly to stop my arms shaking with adrenaline. I was cursing inside my head now, furious with myself for doing something so bloody stupid.

The guards leapt into action. They seemed to move too fast for me to track, never mind get a decent lock onto. After a few futile efforts I muttered, "Sod this," and put one silenced round into the tea urn suspended above the fire.

The high-velocity round ripped through the metal container. It split apart, sending a gush of steaming tea cascading down onto the flames and dousing them almost at once.

The light given out by the fire snapped off as if someone had thrown a blanket over it. Not only that, but the water produced clouds of smoke that stung their eyes and clawed at their throats. The scene through my night scope cleared and sharpened. I saw the guards stumble as their own ability to see was compromised.

And because of that, I saw the figure with the knife flow up out of the terrain behind one of the men, engulfing him in much the way the water had engulfed the fire, washing him down and back. He struggled briefly, then went limp, allowing the AK to be plucked from slack fingers.

The man who'd been alongside him, less than a couple of meters away, never realised anything was amiss until his comrade's gun was turned against him. A short burst later he, too, lay dead on the ground.

The other guards who'd been near the fire had dived for cover behind rocks at the edge of the camp that were large enough to shield them completely. Muzzle flash streaked over the top of the rocks, but I couldn't get a line on the men behind. After a moment I realised they were crouched down, firing blindly over their heads without bothering to aim.

The next time a barrel appeared, I took a careful bead on it and loosed another single round. I saw the AK buck violently as the wooden fore grip shattered in the man's hands. He threw down the useless weapon and ran blindly into the darkness, injured arm cradled to his chest.

I let him go.

The silence that rolled in after the short sharp gunfight was exaggerated by the contrast. Shadows emerged and solidified, moving slow and cautiously. I centred on each one, checking off their identity before moving on.

Ginger and Sporty were easy to spot. They still had their full gear and NVGs. Somehow I was not surprised to find that it was the Special Forces sergeant, Scary, who had dispatched the two Taliban guards with such deadly efficiency. Tate came edging out from cover

Ginger's voice in my ear called me in. I rose stiffly, walked towards the camp with the L115 heavy in my arms. I didn't want to look at the crumpled remnants of the second tent—the one where Posh and Brookes had been held—but like a bad smash on the opposite side of a motorway, somehow I couldn't quite tear my gaze away.

It was Sporty who moved in close, though, who scuffed about with the toe of his boot and lifted folds of canvas with the end of the muzzle.

"You didn't think we were still in there, did you?" asked a voice. We turned. Posh appeared from the direction of the rocks. There was a combat survival knife in his hands and as he spoke he wiped the blade clean on a piece of rag.

"Where the fuck did you get to, mate?" Sporty demanded.

Posh jerked his head back the way he'd come. "Oh, just cleaning up after you, as usual," he said. He held the knife up as if inspecting a blade he must hardly have been able to see. "Took care of your stragglers."

"Where's Brooksy?"

The question had been on my lips but Tate beat me to it. I shut my mouth again and tried to steel myself for the answer.

"He's back there," Posh said, nodding towards the rocks again.

I ran, stumbling, rounded the rocks and froze.

There was a man lying on his back, limbs jittering in a way I'd seen before, when the conscious mind has ceased to provide instructions and what's left is instinct and a nervous system, winding down.

A figure bent over the dying man, hands at his throat. My heart launched into my own throat as my feet took me forward.

Then I faltered as what I was seeing was finally decoded by my brain.

The dying man was not Brookes. He was Taliban, from his dress. It was the figure leaning over him who was in standard Multi-Terrain Pattern combat gear. And the hands he had to the man's neck were not strangling him, as I'd first feared, but doing their best to stem the blood flow from a gaping throat wound.

Brookes looked up, the head torch he was using flaring in my night-sight goggles. I flinched and shut my eyes.

"Sorry," he said, automatically, looked down again at his patient. "I…I've lost him." He let go and sat back on his heels, defeated. "*Fuck.*"

"If it makes you feel any better," Posh said, "if he'd lived we'd have had to kill him anyway."

"No, as a matter of fact," Brookes said, weariness in his voice, "it doesn't make me feel any better at all, thanks."

"Wait a moment. Can we back up a few steps? How the hell did the pair of you get out of that bloody tent?"

"Move first, talk later," the sergeant, Scary, said abruptly. "Find your gear and grab your horses. It'll start getting light in a few hours and, trust me, we want to be *long* gone from here by then."

16

"A mate of mine's a copper," Brookes said. "Last time I was home on leave, he was telling me about some teenage toe-rags he arrested for breaking and entering. He and his oppo nabbed a bunch of them—enough that they ran out of standard handcuffs and had to use the PlastiCuffs type on the rest."

We were heading back towards the village where the local chief had welcomed and then betrayed our advance party. I wondered what kind of a reception we'd receive when we got there this time. Meanwhile, listening to the corporal's story was a good way of taking my mind off what might be to come.

We were both riding one horse and leading another. Scary had insisted we take whatever spare mounts were left with us. Better than leaving them tethered in the middle of nowhere or turning them loose. He had visions of them returning to their home base and raising the alarm. I didn't think it worth mentioning that in my experience most horses did not have the homing instinct—nor the brains, in most cases—of the average pigeon.

Brookes, like the others, had been knocked about by his captors, but nevertheless he wanted to check everyone else over before we moved off. Scary overruled him, on the grounds that we needed to put as much distance between us and what remained of the camp before the survivors who'd fled into the night regrouped, or the rest of the Taliban contingent returned.

So, I rode alongside him on Mones. The little chestnut jogged and pulled faces at the horse I was leading, occasionally laying back his ears and bunching his hindquarters to show he was boss. So much for giving him a name that meant 'friend'.

"Anyway, they put the bigger lads in the steel handcuffs, although the plastic ones have a hell of a breaking strain," Brookes went on. "He said they never thought for a moment any of them would get loose."

"But they managed it."

He nodded. "The smallest, puniest one did. He was out of them in less than a minute. Turned out he untied the laces on his trainers, threaded the ends through the cuffs and reknotted them. Then all he had to do was pump his feet up and down, yeah? The laces built up enough friction to melt through the plastic, and he was off like a rocket."

"He got away?"

Brookes laughed. "Nah, the daft sod forgot he'd tied his laces together. Tripped over his own feet before he'd made it ten yards and fell flat on his face."

"I assume they secured him with something a bit stronger second time around?"

"Had to use another pair of PlastiCuffs—they didn't have anything else—but they made all of them give up their shoelaces."

I grinned at him. "And you did the same thing in the tent—sawed through the zip ties, I mean, rather than falling flat on your face?"

"Yeah." He ducked his head in the direction of Posh, riding up ahead with Scary alongside him. "He was just finding us a way out of the back of the tent when the guards started kicking off."

I laughed out loud, aware as I did so that I was more amused by the story than I should have been. The relief at still being alive—at all of us still being alive—made the story seem funnier. On the eastern horizon the first flush of new day was beginning to dawn, the colours brighter and the smells more vivid than they seemed the day before.

Ahead, Scary wheeled his horse and circled back to us.

"You OK?"

I wasn't sure which of us the question was aimed at, but I gave a wary nod. "I could ask you the same question."

"Oh, don't you worry about me. This is all in a day's work for me," he said, unsmiling. "But I understand you had a bit of a wobble back there."

Reminded of my involuntary yell, I flushed and threw a quick glare in the direction of Sporty and Ginger. They'd both dropped back far enough to be immune to my best hard stare, even if they'd been paying attention.

"I know it's hard to watch and do nothing," Scary said. He slid his gaze sideways over me. "Harder still to act, sometimes."

"I *did* act," I said, keeping my voice even.

He made no reply, just rode alongside me for a few paces, face giving nothing away.

Eventually, I let out an exasperated sigh. "What—you think I should have fired at those two guys before they ever got a shot off, and to hell with the rules of engagement?"

"As soon as they picked up their weapons and moved towards our guys, then as far as I'm concerned unarmed prisoners were in 'imminent danger' and all bets were off. You should have known that, Charlie."

"Should I?" I threw back. "Maybe I'm not used to bending the rules as much as you are, sergeant. And maybe I'd be given a damn sight less leeway if I did."

To my surprise, he nodded. "So you decided their tea kettle was posing an immediate threat to life, did you, and shot that out instead?"

"Have you ever tried that *kahwah* stuff? Half a cupful and you fall into a diabetic coma. Definitely a threat."

"Ah, when you put it like that..."

I sighed, sobered. "Look, I wasn't prepared to kill them in cold blood and I didn't know what else to aim for that would have any effect." I scowled at him. "No doubt you would have done things very differently, of course."

"Probably would have," he allowed. He regarded me stonily for another beat, then a smile snuck all the way across his face. "I have to say, though, you may have shrieked like a girl, but I'll call it a battle cry and let you off, because putting out their campfire like that...well, I never would have thought of it in a million years, but it was fucking inspired."

With a last nod, he nudged his horse into a jog trot and rejoined Posh in front, leaving me staring after him with my mouth open.

"Bloody hell," I said after a moment. "Is it just me, or was that actually faint praise?"

Brookes grinned in response. "From him, I get the feeling that was as close as you're going to get to a standing ovation."

17

I'd been expecting one prisoner. Scary and Posh, ever the over-achievers, came back with three. When they returned from the village to our current location in the hills just above, they not only had the elderly Afghani chief with them, but also two other men I didn't recognise.

Mind you, it's hard to recognise anyone when they have torn strips of fabric bound across their eyes, obscuring half their faces. I only knew the chief by his clothing and the amount of greying beard trailing out beneath his blindfold.

The other two, judging from what bits of scrappy beard I could see, were much younger. The harsh conditions of this country tended to batter anyone into early-onset old age before they were thirty. Still, something about their clothing rang a bell. They'd certainly been present when our guys had been handed to the Taliban. But then, so had half the village.

"Was there a 'buy one, get two free' offer going there or something, pal?" Ginger asked Scary.

Scary shrugged. "It was either grab the lot or abort."

When he yanked the blindfold away from the chief's eyes, the man allowed himself a moment of naked panic before a kind of calm acceptance overtook him. On his knees, with hands tied behind him, he must have already come to terms with his fate.

Scary and Posh had gone in just before sunrise, timing their snatch raid just as the old man finished his *fajr* morning prayers. By the time anyone was likely to have realised he and the other two men were missing, they were all long gone.

From what Ginger let slip, the village chief, Zameer, was a veteran of the *Mujahideen*, the ragged bunch of disparate Islamic fighters who'd taken up arms against the Soviet invasion of 1979 and battled one of the world's superpowers to humiliating stalemate during a decade of conflict.

Now, the skinny old man faced Scary, who was managing to live up to his nickname without overt threats of any kind. He stood watching Zameer with impassive eyes, arms folded across his chest. Tate was at his shoulder, ready to translate.

When the faces of the other two prisoners were uncovered, they proved younger than I'd initially thought—little more than teenagers. They kept their heads bowed, as if by avoiding eye contact they might pretend somehow that this was not happening and we did not exist.

The Spec Ops boys loomed around them, ready to quell any display of resistance. The rest of us stayed close enough to listen, far enough away to keep an eye on our perimeter.

Sooner or later, someone would miss them.

And then they'd come looking.

"You betrayed us," Scary said to the chief, via Tate.

Zameer denied it, but without conviction.

"You handed us over to the Taliban, knowing what they would do with us."

"He reckons he didn't have a choice," Tate said.

Scary glanced at him. "Don't give it to me second-hand—I don't want your interpretation of what he says. I want his *exact* words. You with me, soldier?"

Tate stiffened and only just prevented himself from coming to attention. "Yes, sarge."

Scary nodded, turned back to Zameer. "There's always a choice."

This time, Tate spoke as if channelling the chief, stumbling at first, then getting into his stride. "You…you do not know these men—what they would do to us."

"Whereas *you* clearly know them very well."

"Of course. Many of them he—er, *I*—fought alongside, like brothers, against the Russian invaders. Still they would kill me, my family, if they knew I had allowed you to be given shelter."

"So you were just protecting your family, were you—both by offering us help and then handing us over? Playing both sides against the middle?"

"Word of your arrival had already reached Al-Ghazi's ears. He knew you were coming. If I had tried to deny it…" Zameer waited for Tate to finish speaking, then shrugged. The shrug spoke volumes.

"But he didn't learn of our mission from you?"

"I risked everything by contacting you. Why would I invite suspicion into my house?"

"Somebody betrayed us, Zameer. If it wasn't you, then who else?"

Zameer's gaze remained resolutely on Scary. A little too resolutely, for my liking. I realised he was trying very hard not to look at either of the two young men who'd been taken captive alongside him.

That alone made me study them more intensely. As if aware of the scrutiny, they shifted on their knees, almost squirming. What *was* it about them…?

I stepped in closer. The nearest of them threw me a sideways glance and tried to cringe further away, as if a glimpse of my face might infect him with something distasteful. Infidel was one thing, clearly, but infidel *and* female were too much for him to bear.

"I remember these two," I said abruptly as the memory unfolded. "They were on the roof—the ones who signalled to the Taliban before you were captured."

Scary regarded me for a moment without comment, then jerked his head to Zameer. "Who are they?"

"One is my nephew, Dil," came the reluctant response. "The other is Ramin…my son."

"You are blessed with a large family," Scary said without apparent sarcasm. "Tell me, did they know we were coming, and what for?"

There was a long pause while Zameer absorbed not only the

question, but the implications that went with it. His shoulders drooped a little as he nodded slowly and murmured his assent.

Scary flicked his head to Sporty and Ginger, who closed in on the two younger men and hauled them to their feet. They had already begun to drag them away before the pair thought to react, to resist.

Zameer half-rose in protest. Scary pushed him back onto his knees. Not rough, but firm enough to discourage a further attempt. The chief's eyes followed the two until they were taken out of sight beyond a rocky outcrop.

"Please," Zameer said. "They are young…foolish."

"They are old enough to fight." The implication was clear.

Old enough to die.

The old man's gaze turned pleading, even if he couldn't quite bring himself to beg. Not yet.

Posh cleared his throat. "Clock's ticking," he said to Scary. "We really don't have time to get into a prolonged bout of haggling. Al-Ghazi could appear at any moment, and when he finds we've flown the coop the first thing he's likely to do is spirit away those engineers."

Scary let his breath out fast down his nose, almost a snort. "Yeah, OK. Let's get this over with."

"Hang on!" It was Corporal Brookes who spoke up. He took a step forward. The two Spec Ops boys paused again and Brookes swallowed. "Look, you can't just…"

"Can't what?"

Brookes flushed. "Can't…you know…well, *kill* them."

Scary straightened, pulled back his shoulders, rotated his neck a fraction, and the slow deliberation of his movements was a threat all by itself.

"Oh?"

"Hey, if he was coming at me with an AK, I'd be the first to slot him straight off, don't get me wrong," Brookes said quickly. "But this—" he gestured to the man's bound hands "—this is an execution."

"Yeah," Scary said, his voice cold and hard. His eyes flickered over me, as if waiting for further protest. It took everything I had to stand still and say nothing. "And what do you think they're going to do to those engineers if we don't get to them first? At least I'll make it quick."

Into the humming silence that followed, Zameer spoke and was quickly translated by Tate.

"The men you speak of—these engineers. They are being held in the mountains. It is a secret place. I have sworn never to reveal it."

Scary seemed to consider this for a moment. "We're not asking you to reveal any secrets," he said. "We just want the men returned safe to their families." He paused, added carefully. "Isn't that what anyone would want, if a relative had been…taken?"

The emphasis was not lost on Zameer. Scary didn't even have to let his gaze drift after the two young men. The chief's head drooped in capitulation.

"If this could be…arranged," he said at last, "you would be…merciful?"

Scary nodded without making any promises out loud, one way or the other. Zameer waited, as if hoping for a firm confirmation he must have known wasn't coming, then he inclined his head. "This will be done."

"How?"

"Release my son, with a message. He can—"

Scary didn't let Tate finish his translation before he cut him off.

"No. Your nephew can carry the message. Your son—he stays with us."

18

"NEXT TIME I'm issued with a set of combats, I swear I'm going to get a size over and line the front with foam padding," I muttered. I was lying on stony ground again, heat leaching up out of the earth and into my body until I was greasy with sweat.

"You could always just put on a few pounds of your own padding," Brookes suggested.

I lifted my cheek away from the stock of the rifle long enough to say, "Up yours, corp."

He laughed, but quietly. The two of us were halfway up what was either a large hill or a small mountain, overlooking the valley floor. Opposite us, down below, what was either a large stream or a small river spilled out onto a plateau caused by some passing glacier aeons ago.

The source of the flow was way up in the mountains, and had gradually cut a deep channel between them on its way to the bottom of the valley. It was now a steep-sided ravine, not unlike the one where the Spec Ops Lynx had crash-landed. The similarities were not lost on me.

Somewhere further up the ravine lay a path that led to the cave where the engineers were being held hostage.

Any more detail than that, we didn't know.

Zameer had sent his nephew, Dil, back to the village with a message for the men holding the engineers. I'd no clue what the message said, but between Scary and Zameer, with Tate as go-between, they'd worked out something that obviously convinced them to co-operate. I gathered that the guards were men from the village rather than hardened Taliban. Everyone subcontracted when shortage of labour demanded, it seemed.

Either way, the captors were more inclined to listen to their village elder than some distant fundamentalist doctrine. They would not allow us to go and fetch the engineers, but would bring them down to more neutral territory. The only thing that worried all of us was time.

If we didn't get clear with our hostages before the Taliban returned with Al-Ghazi in tow we'd be up to our necks in the brown smelly stuff. This had already taken longer than any of us had envisaged spending out in the field.

Besides anything else, if it came to a choice between supporting us—foreigners who were here one day and gone the next—and jihadi brothers who were somewhat closer to home, it didn't take a genius to work out where their loyalties would have to lie.

Hadn't Zameer already proved that?

It had taken us a morning to reach this place, and it would take us another half a day to get to our safe extraction zone. Unless we were prepared to ride our borrowed horses into the ground. I was possibly the only one who didn't fancy that option. Already I was fretting about what might happen to my faithful little mount, Mones, after we'd gone.

For now, we had left some of the horses on the other side of the mountain under Posh's watchful eye. He was also guarding Zameer's son, Ramin. Both horses and prisoner were tethered, to one degree or another.

"Here we go," Brookes murmured from behind binoculars. "Movement to the north. Our guys, by the looks of it. Hang on, no—there's only four of them."

I shifted position, swivelling the L115 on its front bipod feet so I could track the arrivals as they picked their way along the side of the river.

It wasn't hard to recognise Scary in the lead. Something about the set of his shoulders, the way he canted his head slightly.

Behind him was Tate, the smallest figure of the bunch, his fatigues subtly different. Then came Ginger, his shock of pale hair and the stubble on his chin bright even under the brim of his hat. Sporty brought up the rear.

"What have they done with Zameer?" I wondered aloud.

"Probably not something we want to know," Brookes said. I felt rather than saw him turn his head to glance sideways at me, considering. "D'you reckon they've slotted him already?"

"That makes it sound like you think it's a foregone conclusion that they're going to," I said, evasive.

He shrugged. "Can they afford to let him go, after what he did before?"

"You heard what he said. He didn't have much of a choice."

"And I heard what Scary's answer was to that as well—that there's always a choice."

"Rather depends on your point of view, doesn't it?"

"So you're happy with it, are you?" he persisted. "If they kill the old man after promising to release him?"

I was glad to have my face up behind the scope, so I didn't have to meet his eye.

"What I think doesn't matter," I said. "It's not my decision to make."

"Ah, the old 'I was only following orders' routine, huh?"

I let my breath out fast in an annoyed spurt. "What do you want me to say?" I demanded. "Either I'm appalled, in which case I'm an emotional female who's not fit to be a frontline soldier, or I say nothing in which case I'm a hard-hearted bitch. Either way, I can't win."

"I spoke up. What does that make me?"

"Ah, but it's different for you. It's part of your job as a medic to save people, as much as it's your job as a soldier to kill them."

"Well, nobody said the path to wisdom was going to be easy, grasshopper."

I sighed, more gently this time. "This is a war zone, and people do things in war they'd never contemplate in a million years otherwise."

"You talking generally now, or personally?"

I said nothing.

After a moment, Brookes said, "Only, you had the opportunity to take out at least a couple of those guys who were holding us, before they had a chance to react. The more of them who survived, the more likely they'd be to go for us. Which was exactly what they *did* do, in fact."

"You mean they tried. *You* were already out of that tent before they shot the shit out of it."

"Yeah, and *you* didn't know that."

OK, he had a fair point there.

"No, I didn't, but I had to trust that you and Posh wouldn't sit there and wait to be rescued—that you'd do your utmost to get yourselves free. So, I did the best I could in the circumstances. The best I could come up with. Sometimes the most effective option is not always the most obvious one."

Whatever Brookes might have been about to say next was cut short by movement along the ravine we were watching. We saw the kicked-up dust before anything else. Then a couple of riders appeared, dressed in the manner I'd come to recognise—baggy *shalwar* trousers and long, loose *kameez* shirts, layered with waistcoats and coats that included everything from old military gear to what looked like a modern ski jacket. They wore an assortment of shapeless headgear, from traditional turban to flat-topped *pakul*, and everything in between. Their horses trotted surefootedly down the narrowest of rocky trails.

They stopped a dozen metres or so from our guys. Tate had halted close to Scary so he could translate for him. Ginger and Sporty pulled out wide onto either flank.

We were way too far away to hear even an echo of the conversation, but I could imagine how it was going. The Afghanis would most likely be asking where Zameer and his son were. Scary, in turn, would want to know about the engineers. A standoff in the making.

For several minutes nothing happened as the talking went on. The horses of the men who'd come down the mountain were skittish in response to the tension of their riders. They stamped and swished their tails and tossed their heads, unsettled. The men spoke with their hands, gesturing in a manner it was difficult to categorise as threatening or friendly.

We watched the group, but both of us also scanned the rocks behind them, looking for the first glimpse of something that didn't look like landscape. Looking for the first sign of a threat.

I don't know what Scary said to the men, but suddenly one of the riders rose in his saddle and waved to some hidden watcher further back up the ravine. I caught the dust rising a moment or two before more horses appeared. I panned across them instantly, slipping my finger inside the trigger guard of the rifle as I checked for weapons raised and ready. Finding none seemed so wrong I went back and checked again.

It took a moment before I processed what I was seeing enough to realise the mounted men approaching were not only unarmed, but they were westerners in civilian dress.

Alongside me, Brookes swore softly under his breath. "I don't bloody believe it," he said. "It's the engineers. Zameer's guys stuck to the bargain."

"Looks that way," I said. "My only worry is, did we?"

19

By the time Brookes and I had scrambled back to where we'd left Posh we were both coated in sweat and grime. My hair clung sodden to the back of my neck, gritty with the dust that was our constant companion. I could feel trickles of clammy moisture dribbling down my spine. I would have sold my soul for a cool shower and some clean underwear.

Posh was already mounted up by the time we reached him. He had his assault rifle slung casually across the front of his saddle, keeping the business end pointing in the direction of Zameer's son, Ramin. The boy had lost the subdued and terrified look he'd worn when first captured and had turned sullen, but with his hands bound in front of him and the reins firmly tied to Posh's own horse, there wasn't much he could do.

"Where's the old man?" I asked, carefully not using Zameer's name in front of his son.

"Oh, he's been all taken care of, don't you worry," Posh said easily.

Brookes paused in the process of untying his horse and stared up at him, shading his eyes against the sun. "'Taken care of'? What the fuck does that mean?"

Posh stared back, a challenge met and matched. "It means he's been taken care of, so shift your arse, corporal. High time we weren't here."

His gaze switched to me, as if to check I wasn't going to voice objections, too.

Part of my brain was refusing to process the possibility that they'd taken the old man away and executed him in cold blood. I tried to keep uppermost the thought that Zameer had delivered four of our number into the hands of Al-Ghazi's men, knowing exactly what the likely outcome of that would be.

When I said nothing, Posh added, "We've had word that Al-Ghazi is on his way. He already knows he's lost one lot of prisoners, and now he's coming for the others."

I'd left the bulky Bowman radio set behind with Posh when Brookes and I took up our position on the other side of the mountain. But I knew the smaller PRRs did not have the range to transmit that information back to Posh from Scary's team. Still, I felt the need to ask:

"How do you know this?"

"From the guards holding the engineers. You'd be amazed what bits of kit they've managed to lay their hands on—not least of which is a decent radio transmitter. Apparently they wanted to make sure we were long gone before Al-Ghazi arrived asking questions."

"Can we get to our extraction point without crossing paths with him?" I asked, keeping my tone level. There were plenty of other questions I could have asked, but those would keep. For now.

Posh raised an eyebrow and waited a moment, as if expecting something I wasn't prepared to add. I kept my mouth shut, turning away to tighten the girth strap holding Mones' saddle before heaving myself aboard.

"It would help if we knew which route they were going to take," he said at last. "It's not like there are many roads in this place, particularly not if you're on four legs instead of four wheels."

"If they're using local villagers as guides, surely they'll stick to the established trails?" I offered.

"So we hope. As it is, we're expecting them to come down the valley from the north—the same way our blokes went in."

"How are Zameer's men going to explain to Al-Ghazi that

they just let us take the engineers?"

"Not our problem," Posh said. "As long as they don't point after us with a cry of 'they went thataway,' they can make up any story they like, as far as I'm concerned."

"Or as long as they don't run into our lot on the way," Brookes said, frowning.

Posh shook his head. "That's why our blokes headed out up the valley to the south. Means we have to take the long way round to reach our evac point, but better that than get into an altercation we don't have the manpower or the firepower to stand a chance of winning."

Posh had already got a GPS fix on our location, and now he took a quick compass bearing for a heading that would converge with Scary and his team. He transmitted a brief message to them using the Bowman, trusting that it would be received.

We set off at a shambling trot. Even that was faster than was prudent on the rocky ground, which dropped away sharply. Ramin's horse, without his hands on the reins to steady him, slipped and slithered. Ramin's face was grim as he gripped tight to the saddle.

As the ground levelled out, I rode up alongside Posh and jerked my thumb back towards our prisoner.

"Why is he still with us?"

"Because we need him."

"What for?"

He flashed me an annoying smile. "Because we do."

"But—"

"Let it go, Charlie. Just take my word for it, all right?"

I wanted to ask if they were planning to 'take care' of him, also, but the words wouldn't come. I nodded, and twitched the reins to turn Mones away from him, circling back to Brookes at the rear. His face reflected my own concerns but neither of us spoke.

Neither of us was happy about what might happen next, but at the same time we were only too aware of the stories. That those who argued too vehemently about human rights' abuses in the field had a nasty habit of not making it back in one piece.

If they made it back at all.

20

WE RODE on for over an hour with no signs of pursuit, but at the same time no sign of Scary, Tate and the others. Posh handed back the Bowman CNR and I sent out frequent, minimal messages *en route*, but either they weren't close enough to respond or weren't there at all. Or, the Bowman wasn't working as it should.

I tried not to think too hard about that possibility.

We'd been weaving through the mountains, skirting the steeper sections while maintaining a rough compass heading. The dust felt like a layer of carpet across the back of my throat. I took constant sips of lukewarm water from my canteen and tried not to fantasise about swigging something long and fruity, and cold enough to make condensation form on the outside of the glass.

The landscape of Helmand around us had a magnificent brutality about it. The largest of Afghanistan's provinces, it was stripped and sparse except around the winding course of the Helmand River, which began in the Bābā Range of the Hindu Kush mountains on the border with Pakistan. It eventually emptied into Lake Hamun in the Sīstān swamp of neighbouring Iran, more than 700 miles later.

I didn't like staying so close to the river as we scribed a huge semicircle to eventually head northwest again for our extraction point. The fertile river valley was where the bulk of the inhabitants of Helmand lived and worked. It made chances of a contact with the enemy too high. Especially when we were split into two groups like this.

I tried the Bowman again. This time I got a broken-up, patchy response. I nudged Mones forward into a messy canter and caught up with Posh. He slowed as I came alongside him, and I sent our call-sign again. The return transmission was still garbled, but at least it was there.

Fifteen minutes later, we made our rendezvous.

Posh nodded to the rest of his team, and Brookes and I grinned at Tate, but that was as much of a reunion as we had time for.

Scary wheeled his horse away and would have ridden on had Brookes not called him back.

"I need to give these guys a quick check over," he said, nodding to the engineers.

Scary's gaze flicked across the men. "They've made it this far with no problems."

"That doesn't mean they'll make it all the way," Brookes said. "Come on, just a quick break. We'll lose more than that if one of them faints and falls off his horse."

Scary hesitated a moment, then nodded. "Ten minutes."

I climbed off Mones, suppressing a groan at my raw seat bones, and went to help the engineers dismount. They struggled to do so with any fluidity, grunting as their boots hit the ground and the shock of the landing jarred up into their body.

Close to, the three men looked weary but far from the exhausted state I'd expected. They were unshaven, but that proved nothing. They might have been bearded before they were taken, and they didn't have the hollowed-out gaze of men who'd been held long enough to forget who they were. In fact, some of them were even tanned, which did not point to a long period of captivity, if it pointed to captivity at all.

Corporal Brookes had grabbed his medical kit and was shining a penlight into their eyes, checking blood pressure, asking about untreated wounds, bouts of sickness or diarrhoea.

Generally, though, I thought they all looked in remarkably good nick after their experience.

Posh was still looming over our prisoner, Ramin. Ginger and Sporty had naturally moved to vantage points to keep watch. I pulled water canteens from the spare horses and offered them round.

The first of the engineers was a slim black guy of indeterminate age, although his beard was flecked through with grey. When I handed him water he took it before doing a double-take, eyes tracking me up and down, as if seeking confirmation that I was indeed female. He wouldn't have got much from my dusty fatigues and boots, and I wore my hair short, so maybe that was the reason for his frown.

"How are you doing?" I asked, just to put him out of his misery if nothing else.

"Ah, OK, I guess."

"You're American?"

"Canadian."

"Sorry. You must get that a lot."

He shrugged and smiled. "It's an easy mistake to make."

"Is that what the Afghanis did—mistook you for Yanks?"

"No, they knew exactly who we were and why we were there," the engineer said.

"Which was?"

He glanced at me sharply, as if that was information I should already have known if I'd any right to.

"We were working on the Grishk Dam. It was built back at the end of World War Two and even if the old turbines were still functioning, they're way outdated. We were sent to look at ways of upgrading them to provide power for this whole area."

"Seems like a bit of a risky proposition, given the current situation here."

"Yeah, well, I don't make the policy, I just have to try to make it work."

"You would have thought that would be something the locals would welcome, not try to sabotage."

He gave another shrug and his lips twisted wryly. "See, now you're just being logical."

"When did they grab you?"

"Few weeks ago? It gets kinda hard to tell." He rubbed a hand over his scalp. "One day runs into another."

"Did they…?" My voice trailed off, unsure how to ask the question.

"Interrogate us? Torture us?" He shook his head. "No, these were not fundamentalists. I got the impression they were just doing a job—minding us like they would their goats or sheep. Not what you might call friendly, but not cruel either. Never even kept us chained up most of the time." He waved a hand to indicate the surrounding landscape. "After all, even if we escaped—on foot, alone out there—where were we gonna go?"

"Minding you for whom? Were they waiting for Al-Ghazi?"

The engineer frowned. "Who's that?"

"Right, that's enough lounging about. We need to keep moving," Scary's voice cut across the conversation. "Anybody needs to take a piss, do it now, because we're not stopping again until nightfall." He glared at me. "You managed to get a response from HQ yet?"

"No, sergeant, not as yet."

"Well, you better keep trying then, hadn't you?"

The sharp tone surprised as much as it angered me. I opened my mouth then took in his scowling features and shut it again, restricting myself to a muttered, "Yes, sergeant."

The engineer handed over the water canteen with eyebrows raised.

"OK, I take it back about the Afghanis not being friendly," he murmured. "Compared to your guy over there, they were a real barrel of laughs."

21

OUR ROUTE MIGHT HAVE SEEMED circuitous, but we crossed into the neighbouring valley without meeting anyone, man or beast. It was mid-afternoon but so far the sun showed no inclination to slacken its grip on the day. The heat had a physical weight. Even the horses began to droop under it, their coats darkening with sweat. The reins creamed it off their necks as lather.

I kept trying the Bowman CNR at regular intervals, requesting our extraction, but I was wary about flattening the battery pack—the life expectancy was nowhere near what the specs claimed. There was still no response. If they could hear me, I couldn't hear them.

Scary left Ginger on point and rode back, nudging his horse into step alongside Mones.

"Still nothing," I said, anticipating his question. "I'll let you know as soon as I make contact."

Scary nodded, and we jogged along in silence for maybe half a dozen strides, then he said, "Spit it out, Charlie. What's on your mind?"

"What happened to Zameer?"

He glanced at me, his gaze assessing, and his tone was entirely neutral. "What do you think happened to him?"

"It's not so much 'think' as a mixture of hope and fear," I said.

"I *hope* you let him go back to his village, because I, for one, believed him when he said he had no choice in what he did."

"But?"

"But, I *fear* you probably slit his throat and left him for the wolves."

We rode in silence for half a dozen strides, the horses' heads nodding in time with each step, before he spoke again.

"I see. And if I did, what would you do about that?"

"Do? Nothing," I said. "I can see how you'd justify it as an operational necessity, even if I didn't agree with you."

"Why not?"

I threw him a quick glance but there was no anger in his face, as there hadn't been in his voice. It seemed that he genuinely wanted to know. Even so, I was wary.

"Because anyone who studies military history realises that appealing to the hearts and minds of the local population is one of the most important factors, especially in a guerrilla war like Vietnam, or here in Afghanistan. Killing off a village elder because he pissed you off is not going to win you allies for the future." My eyes drifted to Zameer's son, still slumped on his horse with hands tied. "It breeds resentment and hatred in the next generation. Fires them up."

"They've got their radical clerics to fire them up," Scary said. "If we cut them some slack, we're seen as weak, and if we *don't*, well, they've already been told we were the spawn of Satan anyway."

"According to Islam, I think you'll find Satan is known as Iblis."

"Whatever. The point is, I'm not here to kill civilians, just as long as they don't try to kill me *or* my team. If they do, then all bets are off."

I shrugged and said nothing. I hardly thought anything I could come up with at this point was likely to change his mind, and this was not the time or place to attempt it. Better to shut the hell up before I gave myself the kind of reputation I could well do without.

Scary's intense gaze stayed on me for a moment longer, one eyebrow raised as if he couldn't quite believe I'd given in so easily. Then he peeled away and called a halt so Sporty and Ginger could recce forward.

As soon as they'd dismounted and headed for the crest of the next hill, Scary moved across to where Posh was leading Ramin's horse and tied a camo scarf across Ramin's mouth. The youth glared at him from over the makeshift gag but did not put up a fight.

"Why do that now?" Brookes asked.

"Just a precaution," Scary told him. "We're getting close to the village. Ideally, I'd like to give it a wider berth, but if we want to get to our HLZ early enough to secure the area, we're already cutting it fine." He glanced at me. "Especially as we haven't yet managed to raise HQ."

He made it sound like I was personally responsible for the Bowman's failings. I stared him down without flinching. It seemed to amuse rather than annoy him.

The Canadian engineer I'd talked to when we made our last stop for water moved his horse closer to Scary. "So, what happens if you *don't* make contact before we're due to be picked up?" he demanded.

Whatever answer Scary might have given him, he never got to utter it. The unmistakable sound of automatic gunfire made us all duck, cursing, and reach for our own weapons. It took a second to realise the rounds were not being aimed at us. They were coming from over the hilltop, from the direction of the village.

22

A FEW MINUTES after Sporty and Ginger went up the hill, they radioed down for Scary to join them. The request, such as it was, was cryptic, but clearly Scary had worked with his guys long enough to read plenty between the lines. He paused, his eyes flicking in my direction as he gave them a murmured affirmative.

"Charlie—with me." He nodded to the L115 hooked onto my saddle. "And bring that with you."

He didn't wait to find out if I followed, just turned on his heel and started up the steep hillside. I jumped down from Mones' back, grabbed the rifle and scrambled to catch up.

As soon as I was close enough to be heard at a whisper I demanded, "What's happening?"

"Al-Ghazi," Scary said sourly. "Looks like he wasn't convinced that the villagers played no part in our escape."

"What's he doing?"

He paused. "You sure you want to know?"

I swallowed, nodded. He looked for a moment like he didn't believe me. Not surprising really. I wasn't sure I believed myself.

We neared the ridge line, went low and crawled into position alongside the two other Spec Ops men.

Below us, the village was too far away to see much detail with the naked eye, but even at this distance I could make out a number of men in the compound of the house where our guys had first met with Zameer. They had herded a group of villagers together and were beating them with long canes or sticks. I guessed the villagers were all women only because they wore the *burqa*. From the faint screams that drifted upwards, it provided no protection—cultural or otherwise.

Children huddled around the women's legs. The men laid into them without mercy, adults and children alike. The sheer effort they were putting into the blows, the power and the force of them, spoke to passion or venom.

My stomach lurched at the sight of it. I tasted bile in my throat, swallowed it down. It left a greasy slither behind my ribcage.

"What the hell are they doing?"

Scary leaned in close and spoke directly into my ear. His voice was soft enough to make me flinch.

"When the Tali first came to power they enforced a particularly hard-line version of *sharia* law. Corporal—and capital—punishment was commonplace for the slightest infraction. So, behold the justice system in action, Afghan style."

"But what are the women and kids supposed to have actually done?"

He shrugged. "Beyond being the property of men they think are traitors? Who knows."

"Aye," Ginger said. "The Tali don't think much of you lot. Chattels, you know."

I didn't respond to that, eyes scanning the buildings, people, and vehicles nearby. Al-Ghazi's men had arrived by truck rather than on horseback. There were two old Toyota Land Cruisers and a six-wheel Russian ZIL-131 truck pulled up in the open area in front of the house where Brookes had gone to treat the young boy who was another of Zameer's nephews. What would happen to him now, I wondered?

There were armed men everywhere. Another concentration of them clustered in the street. Then one moved and I caught a glimpse of something bundled at his feet. Not quite trusting my eyes, or my imagination, I quickly folded out the L115's bipod legs, settled it, and uncapped the scope.

As I put my eye to it, the scene came into sharp focus. A man was on the ground, but it was now clear that I could see his body only from the waist up. At first I'd feared what I was looking at might be only *part* of a man, dismembered. My belief that people die neat and tidy and in one piece, culled from watching too many TV detective shows, had not survived my first close encounter with a roadside explosive device out here.

But as I watched, I realised the man wasn't *on* the ground.

He was in it.

His legs and lower torso, including his hands and forearms, were buried in the trampled earth. His clothing was torn, his face bloodied. It took me a moment or two to realise who it must be.

"But that's…Zameer," I said dumbly. I looked to Scary, almost reproachful. "You didn't kill him."

"No, more fool me, I didn't."

"Should'a slotted him while you had the chance," Sporty commented dryly. "At least you would've made it quick, eh?"

There were a lot of questions I could have asked—should have asked—but the time for that might come later. "What are they going to do to him?"

"Stone him to death—or make his family and friends do it for them," Scary said, nothing in his voice. "Probably tomorrow, or the next day—if the heat and dehydration doesn't do the job for them."

"So, what's the plan?" I asked, glancing at their set faces. "How do we do this?"

"How do we do what?" Sporty demanded.

I resisted the urge to grind my teeth. "How do we get him out of there?"

"We don't," Scary said flatly.

"You mean you're not even going to *attempt* to do anything? You have to be kidding me!"

"Charlie, there are seven of us, plus three civilians and one prisoner, against probably thirty-five or forty experienced Tali fighters. We're weapons light and time poor. What the fuck do you suggest we do?"

"Suggest?" I repeated, trying to keep both outrage and volume from my voice. "I don't know. You're the experts. But I sure as hell know what I suggest we *don't* do, which is to leave him at the mercy of those bastards!"

"'Course not," Ginger said. He flicked me a quick assessing look I failed to interpret fully. "That's where you come in."

"Me?"

"Yeah. You've already proved you can hit a target at around seven hundred metres, and the suppressor means they won't be able to pinpoint a single shot."

"Wait a minute. You surely don't expect—?"

"Yeah," Scary repeated, and the grim smile on his face made me realise he'd laid a neat trap for me, and I'd walked straight into it. "You don't want to leave Zameer to be tortured to a slow and painful death at the hands of Al-Ghazi, so here's something you *can* do about it. Kill him."

23

"ONE ROUND STRAIGHT through his mouth and you take out the brain stem," Ginger said. "He'll never know what hit him."

"Surely, there's got to be another way."

"If you can suggest one, I'm all ears." Scary's gaze settled on me. I wondered why I hadn't noticed before that his eyes were so dark they were almost black. Like his soul? I shook my head a little, trying to rattle out such fanciful imaginings.

"If he was one of your own men, would this still be your best solution?" I demanded. Nobody spoke. "No, I thought not."

"If it was me facing the same thing, I'd be praying one of you had the guts to pull the trigger and have done with it," Ginger said bluntly. "Better than the alternative, eh?"

"It's still nowhere near as good as being rescued, is it?"

"We don't have the resources," Scary said, more weary than exasperated.

"What about Al-Ghazi?"

"What about him?"

"If we took him out instead, would the others kill Zameer anyway or fall back?"

"Depends," Scary said. "If they thought Zameer was in any way to blame, then they'd probably wipe out the whole village. If not...I don't know. Irrelevant, in any event."

Something in me couldn't resist goading him. "I thought Al-

Ghazi was your 'high-value target'? I thought half the reason for this bloody mission in the first place was to grab him. Surely it's better if you eliminate him rather than simply let him go?"

Scary shrugged. "Maybe, maybe not. He's an identified and identifiable player. Take him out and who knows who might rise up to take his place. If it's somebody we have no intel on, we could be taking one step forwards and two back."

"Better the devil you know, is that it?" I asked sourly.

"I don't like it any more than you do, but I'm a realist."

He started to shuffle backwards, away from the scene below. I wasn't about to let him off that easily.

"If you were planning on snatching Al-Ghazi, somebody else would have had to take his place anyway, wouldn't they?"

He paused, only for a moment. "Yeah, but that would have been more than compensated for by whatever info we managed to squeeze out of him."

"He must be important, this guy. After all, you were prepared to risk everything—even going on with half your men dead or injured—to get your hands on him. You sure you want to give up on that now, when he's right there?"

Scary threw me a warning glare that said he knew exactly what I was trying to do, and what he thought of the attempt. It wasn't complimentary. I didn't care.

Reckless now, I ploughed on. "What's lost by exploring the possibilities?"

"Time we may not have," Scary snapped.

"Which one *is* Al-Ghazi, for a start?"

It was Ginger who spoke. "He's inside Zameer's place."

"OK, so if you *were* going to extract him from there, how would you go about it? Hypothetically speaking, of course."

"For someone who hates being patronised," Scary bit out, "you do a fucking good job of it yourself."

I grinned at him. "Yeah, irritating, isn't it?"

There was a long pause, then Ginger said diffidently, "At least we've been inside the house ourselves, so we know the layout—ground floor, anyway."

"And we might get some info out of matey-boy back there,

too," Sporty said, jerking his head in the direction of the still-bound-and-gagged Ramin.

"Oh, don't you fucking start—!"

Scary's growl was cut short, tense. My eyes swivelled back to the scope, skimming across the scene below. There was movement in the doorway of Zameer's house that made me stop scanning abruptly. I tracked instead as a man stepped out, tugging a boy by one arm.

The kid must have been six or seven. He didn't look good. His skin was pale with a waxy tint and there were dark circles under his eyes. His neck seemed too slender to support his head, and his hair was unevenly flattened and tufted by restless friction, like he'd just been taken from his bed.

I lifted my head. "Is that—?"

"Zameer's nephew—another of his nephews—yes," Scary said tightly. "The one Brookes treated last time we were here."

"What's he going to do to the kid?"

"Kill him in front of Zameer? Make him pull the trigger? Hand him the first rock? How the fuck should I know?"

I could hear the frustration as well as the anger in Scary's voice, and this time it wasn't directed towards me.

He glanced at Sporty. "Bring Ramin up—quietly. Let's see what he can tell us once he's seen what they're about."

Sporty nodded and slithered away hardly making a sound. Thirty seconds later he was back, forcing Ramin down low alongside us. The gag was gone, although his hands were still tied. Sporty held a combat knife almost casually at his throat, just in case he thought about doing something brave, or stupid.

"Ask him—" Scary began, then stopped. "Shit, where's Tate?"

"I...speak English," Ramin said with obvious reluctance.

"Kept that quiet, didn't you?" Scary muttered. He pointed. "You see what Al-Ghazi is planning on doing to your father? And your little cousin?"

Ramin's sharply indrawn breath answered for him.

"If we try to stop Al-Ghazi, will your people help us, or try to kill us?"

"I will help you."

"Not quite the answer I was looking for," Scary muttered, "but it's a start."

"Most cover to the northwest. We can get to within fifty metres before we have to make a break," Sporty put in.

"Tate can spot for her, and we'll take the medic, eh?" Ginger said, his mind already bouncing ahead. At Scary's nod, he and Sporty eased backwards and disappeared down the slope, taking Ramin with them.

He didn't want to leave his vantage point, as if he couldn't bear to tear his eyes away from the unfolding events, and what was about to happen to his father. Al-Ghazi had now pulled the boy out into the street. When the youngster stumbled and almost fell, I felt my breath hitch at what might come next.

But Al-Ghazi bent and lifted the boy easily into his arms, settling him on one hip with all the ease of a natural father. I could see them talking intently, their heads bent close together. Whatever the man said must have reassured the youngster, because his struggles ceased and he wrapped his arms around the man's neck, hanging on.

When they reached the open area where Zameer was half-buried in the dirt, Al-Ghazi twisted so that the boy could look down on his uncle. Zameer began to thrash in the dirt, trying to get loose. He was not successful.

"You may still have to take out Zameer, if they start on him," Scary said. "Trust me, it'll be an act of mercy."

"And if Al-Ghazi makes a move on the boy before you're in position?"

Scary's face hardened. "Then kill the fucker," he said. "Think you can do that?"

I nodded, hoping he wouldn't see the hesitation. He looked about to ask again when Tate scrambled up next to us and his attention was diverted into instructions that Tate should spot for me.

"What, from here?"

"No," Scary said. "I want you to move back to that far ridge."

Tate's eyes followed the finger pointed in the direction of another mountainside, eyebrows climbing. "Jeez, that's got to be another three or four hundred metres."

His estimate was probably about right. We were already close to five hundred metres from the village. I knew the extra distance would test me in all kinds of ways, but Scary brushed aside Tate's protest. "She's proved she can shoot at that range."

"Even so—"

"Stay here and they'll blast the pair of you before she's got a second shot off. Move back, and we're planning to keep them too occupied to set up a decent response, even if they could get close enough."

Tate threw me a dirty look, and I knew he was remembering the fact I could have shot the guards around the campfire after he and the others were taken prisoner, but had not done so. "Yeah, she *can*. Question is, *will* she?"

"Cut that out," Sporty told him. "It's part of your job to make sure she does, mate."

Tate's hands tightened reflexively around his assault rifle and for a moment I wondered how exactly he intended to carry out that order.

IT TOOK us sixteen minutes to reach a suitable sniper's nest, on the crest of the far ridge with large enough rocks around us to shelter behind and conceal our silhouette. There was a downward slope at our backs to cover a withdrawal that I could only hope wouldn't turn into an all-out retreat.

It took another two minutes for my pulse to stabilise enough that I thought I stood a chance of hitting anything I aimed at.

Tate called for a sit-rep. I recognised Ginger's voice over my headset.

"Too many X-rays," he said. "If we're going to do this quietly, we gotta take him inside the house."

"Roger that," Scary acknowledged. "Charlie, do you have eyes on the target?"

"He's still in the open, and still holding the boy."

"Roger that. If we have to abort, do you have a clear shot?"

Through the scope, I could see Al-Ghazi plainly. But he had his left side facing me, and the boy was on his right hip. As he shifted his feet, I caught occasional glimpses of the kid's face directly behind his head.

The L115 was loaded with .338 Lapua Magnum rounds that left the muzzle at a velocity in excess of nine hundred metres a second. The gun had an effective range of fifteen hundred metres. Passing through a human skull, even at somewhere over eight hundred metres distance, would not significantly slow the projectile.

Certainly nowhere near enough to stop it going straight through another, smaller, head, so close to the first.

"Negative," I said. "I have no clear shot."

Below, in the village, the crowd was moving, bunching together, almost being herded towards the open area and Zameer. It didn't take a genius to work out the show was about to begin. Al-Ghazi showed no signs of heading back to the house, and I guessed he wouldn't now until it was all over.

Until it was all too late.

Scary's voice came over the net sharp with tension. "If you want to do anything about this, Charlie, you're out of time."

"Christ," I muttered, twitching my sights between the old man buried up to his chest, and the man with the boy on his hip.

"What are you waiting for? Take the shot. Take the fucking shot!"

24

"WHAT ARE YOU WAITING FOR? Take the shot. Take the fucking shot!" It was Sporty's voice I could hear.

"She's not up to it," Tate muttered. "I told you she wouldn't be."

"Shut up, for fuck's sake. Charlie, listen to me. Can you confirm you have eyes on the target?"

I lifted my face from the adjustable cheek piece on the stock of the rifle and blinked away sweat caused partly by the heat, and partly by a mix of adrenaline and fear. I could still feel the impression of the pad against my skin. I'd been leaning into it so hard all my teeth felt pushed out of line.

I was bedded-in behind the gun, and calculated that I was approximately eight hundred and seventy metres from my target. With the sun over my left shoulder, in good cover, there was little chance anyone in the village would see or hear the first shot.

It wasn't that which stayed my hand.

The Schmidt and Bender scope was good for up to two thousand metres. At this distance the man who was my intended target showed up pin-sharp and gin-clear. Maybe *that* was the problem.

He stood holding the child, with a group of his men clustered loosely around him. They were laughing, at ease and unsuspecting. I could tell from the body language that they respected him as much as they feared him. Something about the way they followed his lead, listened attentively when he spoke, nodding and smiling with anticipated approval.

He seemed close enough that I could see the weave of his clothing, the stubble on his face, a lattice of burn scars on the side of his neck. He was human and breathing, no longer an abstract series of equations involving range, elevation, and windage.

Scary's voice was low and quiet in my ear. "I repeat: can you confirm you have eyes on the target?"

I swallowed. The fine desert dust coated my teeth.

"Affirmative."

"He's just a target, Charlie. Don't think of him as anything but that. Remember what he's done, what he's about to do, and not what he's doing right now, OK?"

"OK."

"You are clear to engage. If it helps, I'll make it a fucking order."

I muttered, "Have that," and nestled my face onto the cheek pad again, flexed my right hand around the pistol grip. The fact the grip was intended for a larger hand, that the shoulder pad had been hastily modified to take my smaller frame into account rammed it home to me, now more than ever, that this was not my weapon. Not my task. That I was not supposed to be here, and there would be hell to pay when the top brass found out.

I took a breath, shut my eyes a moment and breathed out, long and slow, willing my heart rate to steady along with my nerves. I tuned out Tate alongside me. He was cursing more loudly now, vibrating with tension and anger.

When I opened my eyes again, Al-Ghazi was still exactly where he had been in my sight picture. He'd turned slightly sideways, though, so I could see more of the boy. There was just a chance any shot I fired at the man might *not* also kill the child.

I curled my forefinger delicately around the trigger.

At that moment Al-Ghazi raised his free arm and signalled to his men. As they began to gather he moved again, and now the boy's body was once more hidden behind his own.

I swore under my breath, as if the boy's safety was my only concern. The only thing holding me back.

One of Al-Ghazi's men jerked the muzzle of his rifle into the ribs of a teenage villager until the youth stooped and, with great reluctance, picked up a rock. As he straightened, I recognised Zameer's nephew, Dil. His face, his eyes, showed a torment that was almost physical. More villagers were forced to do the same, forming a rough circle around where the old man was half-buried. Al-Ghazi stood and watched, talking to the boy he held, their foreheads close to touching.

Just behind him, visible in the reticle of the scope, several of his men who were not tasked with cajoling the villagers climbed into the back of the six-wheel Russian truck they'd brought with them. It had planked side boards and a canvas tilt on a hooped frame. I shifted my aim, my focus. One of the men pushed back the tilt and they began shifting the cargo. As they turned, struggling with the weight in the awkward space, I saw what that cargo was.

And before I could second-guess my decision or my motives, I squeezed the trigger and took the shot.

EPILOGUE

"ON THE BACK of the truck were about a dozen thirty-pound propane cylinders," I said, keeping my voice even, my tone neutral. "I fired at them."

"Why? Were you hoping for an explosion?"

The man asking the questions wore the pip and crown of a lieutenant colonel on each shoulder, but no regimental insignia. He hadn't given a name at the start of this interview, and I knew better than to ask for one.

The two officers flanking him were familiar, though. On his left was my CO, scowling. On his right was Captain MacLeod. He didn't look much happier.

All three were seated at a table with files and folders and notes spread in front of them that I was not close enough to read. I remained standing, having been marched into the room as if to courts martial.

"I thought that unlikely, sir. There was no flame to cause ignition, and I was using standard ammunition, not tracer or incendiary rounds."

"So, what *was* the reason for this...*unusual* choice of target?"

Was that a hint of sarcasm slipping into the cracks of his question? It was hard to tell. I tried not to let it rattle me.

"I wanted to prevent the imminent deaths of Zameer and his nephew, without giving away my position or endangering the lives of the other villagers. I also wanted to give the Special Forces team the opportunity to snatch their target, so I needed to create a viable diversionary tactic, sir."

"And shooting at gas bottles you knew were *not* going to explode was what you came up with?"

"Yes, sir." I swallowed. "I knew the rounds would go straight through and out the other side. I, ah, saw it done once on the ranges. Because the gas is so highly pressurised, when it's suddenly released like that you tend to get a kind of violent cart-wheeling effect. I reasoned that having several steel cylinders weighing thirty pounds apiece suddenly flipping up into the air might just…distract them a bit."

"Indeed," the lieutenant colonel said. His voice was devoid of emotion now. I couldn't get a read on him one way or another. "And then?"

"Once we'd confirmed that the team had achieved their objective we made a tactical withdrawal to the rendezvous point with them and our transport—"

"Your horses?"

When the Chinook landed to pick us up I could still remember the surprise on Ramin's face as Scary had not only let him loose but told him to keep the animals. Seems like he hadn't needed my lecture about winning hearts and minds. He was already way ahead of me.

"Yes, sir. Then we headed for the HLZ and were brought back to Camp Bastion. We—Corporal Brookes, Private Tate and myself —were kept quarantined from the rest of our unit. This morning we were put on a Hercules back to Brize Norton and now…here I am, sir."

"Indeed," the lieutenant colonel said again, only now he was frowning. "Well, soldier, you got yourself caught up in an operation that was highly classified and is likely to remain so. You are not to discuss any of the details outside this room, with *anyone*. Do I make myself clear?"

"Yes, sir."

"Even with the other members of your unit who were there with you—nobody. Understood?"

"Yes, sir," I repeated.

He nodded, gaze dropping to his notes. "Very well. That will be all."

I stiffened to attention, muttered, "Yes, sir. Thank you, sir." But then I hesitated when I knew I should just do a smart about-face and march straight out of there.

"Was there something else, Charlie?" It was Captain MacLeod who asked. I flicked my eyes in his direction and found his expression just unbending enough to give me courage.

"Sir…am I…?" I swallowed again. "That is to say, sir, have I done something I might be facing charges for?"

My CO scowled some more and opened his mouth, no doubt to lambast me, but the lieutenant colonel cut him off sharply.

"Charges? What makes you ask that? Do *you* think you've done something wrong?"

"I'm not sure, sir. I'm not sure if I've done too much, or not enough."

He sat back in his chair, eyebrows raised.

I tried to work up some spit in my mouth, glanced down at the bulled toecaps of my boots as if hoping to see inspiration reflected in their shiny depths. *Ah well, may as well be hanged for a sheep as a lamb.* I straightened my shoulders.

"I don't know if there were times I should have engaged, and didn't. And other times when I probably exceeded my remit, sir."

The lieutenant colonel let out a snort. "Soldier, you exceeded your remit from the moment you became a part of that operation," he said, his voice like a cracked whip. "The British Army does not—and to this point never has—put its female personnel into forward combat situations. At some point in the future that may change, but at the moment it is entirely against the regulations, as you no doubt well know?"

"Yes, sir."

"'Yes, sir.' And yet you agreed to go into hostile territory in the role of *sniper* for a Special Forces team who were already well aware they had been compromised, and that the likelihood of capture was proportionally increased."

"They made no secret of the risks, sir. Neither did Captain MacLeod. And I did volunteer, sir."

"Hm, yes, so I understand, but that's beside the point. The

fact remains that Captain MacLeod should not have allowed you the *option* to volunteer." He leaned forwards, resting his forearms on the tabletop. "Is *that* clear?"

"Yes, sir."

He held my eyes for a moment longer, then nodded. "How*ever*," he said, drawing out the word. "I have read the debrief from my team, and heard the verbal reports from Brookes and Tate about the manner in which you conducted yourself out there."

I heard a voice in the back of my head going, *"Uh-oh."*

"It would seem," the lieutenant colonel went on, "that you showed extraordinary levels of marksmanship under fire, as well as considerable initiative in your selection of targets. This not only saved the lives of your fellow soldiers but also led to the successful capture of a high-value enemy asset when it might have seemed that our only option was to eliminate him, with all the loss of potential intelligence that entailed."

"Um, yes, sir," I said faintly.

He allowed himself the ghost of a smile. "So, Charlie, is it? No, you will certainly *not* be facing any charges, if that puts your mind at rest?"

"Yes, sir. It does."

"Good." He nodded again. "You're dismissed."

I snapped to attention, executed an about-face of parade ground quality, and stomped out, my boots echoing very loud on the polished wooden floor.

Out in the corridor, I finally slumped against a wall and ran my hands over my face. It was no surprise to find I was sweating.

"Scary in there, was it?" asked a voice.

I jerked upright, found myself facing the Special Forces sergeant we'd given just that nickname to. He was leaning on a doorway opposite, in black jeans and a donkey jacket, and looking no less dangerous for being out of uniform.

"Scary out here, too," I blurted before I could stop myself.

He gave me a puzzled frown. "Oh?"

It must have been the relief at making it out of that room alive that made me light-headed and loose-lipped. As we headed for the exit I explained, finally, about how we'd nicknamed him and his team after the Spice Girls.

I wasn't sure how he'd take it, but he actually laughed. "I'll let them know," he said. "Only, I think I'll tell Ben you dubbed him Baby rather than Sporty. Otherwise there'll be no living with his ego. We can hardly prise him out of the gym as it is."

We pushed through the double doors leading to the outside world. The air was cold and crisp, with the smell of dead leaves that marks a turning season. It seemed a long way from the unrelenting heat of Helmand.

"So they were OK with you in there?" he asked as we moved down the steps and paused, the way two people do when they're about to head off in opposite directions and they know this is goodbye.

"Yeah," I said. "At least I'm not in trouble." I thought of my CO's glowering face and amended that to, "Well, not much, anyway."

"Trouble?" He seemed genuinely surprised. "Christ, Jesus, if you were one of the lads they'd be pinning a medal on you."

"And here was I thinking I'd done well not to get booted out for it."

He was silent for a moment. I stood waiting and tried not to shiver. It seemed bloody cold back in England.

"I never really got a chance to ask you," he said then, "just before you hit those gas bottles, what went through your mind?"

I stared at him blankly. "It was the way Al-Ghazi was holding the boy," I said at last. "Like…he had sons of his own. I took a chance that, when something happened, he'd try to get him to somewhere safe—like back inside Zameer's house."

The corner of his mouth twitched slightly. "And there was I thinking you were being squeamish again."

I smiled and avoided giving him an answer to that one. "It worked, didn't it?"

"Oh yeah. Which is why, although *officially* they may be pretending this never happened, *unofficially* you want to take full advantage, before they forget exactly what you did."

"Take advantage how?"

"There's talk of allowing an intake of female soldiers to try their hand at Selection."

"What—for the SAS?"

"For Special Forces, in whatever specialty best suits your abilities. Tell them you want to put your name forward." At my look of disbelief, he turned towards me, too close, and suddenly he'd slipped straight back into the skin he'd worn in Afghanistan. It was all I could do not to take a step back from him. "I'm serious. You've just more than proved yourself in a combat situation, not some training exercise. That's not something they can easily ignore."

"You reckon?"

"I know. You've got a lot going for you. Don't let them tell you any different."

"I won't. And thank you…I don't even know your name. Or is that classified?"

"Not anymore." His eyes were very dark, almost black, and he hardly seemed to blink. It was unnerving. "It's Sean," he said. "Sean Meyer."

He held out his hand and we shook. It seemed absurdly formal under the circumstances. Considering what we'd been through.

"Thank you again, Sean."

"You're welcome, Charlie. Don't forget what I said."

"I won't."

"Good," he said, turning up the collar of his jacket against the autumn chill. "Because I won't forget you."

AFTERWORD

Liked it?
If you've enjoyed this book, there is no greater compliment you can give an author than to leave a review on the retailer site where you made your purchase, or on social media. Doesn't have to be long or in great detail, but it means a huge amount if you'd write a few words to say what you liked about it, and encourage others to give my work a try. Thank you so much for taking the time.

I'm only human...
We all make mistakes from time to time. This book has gone through numerous editing, copyediting, and proofreading stages before making it out into the world. Still, occasionally errors do creep past us. If by any chance you do spot a blooper, please let me, the author, know about it. That way I can get the error corrected as soon as possible. Plus I'll send you a free digital edition of one of my short stories as a thank you for your eagle-eyed observational skills! Email me at **Zoe@ZoeSharp.com**.

Please Note
This book was written in British English and UK spellings and punctuation have been used throughout.

ABOUT THE AUTHOR

Zoë Sharp opted out of mainstream education at the age of twelve and wrote her first novel at fifteen. She created her award-winning crime thriller series featuring ex-Special Forces trainee turned bodyguard, **Charlotte 'Charlie' Fox**, after receiving death threats in the course of her work as a photojournalist. She has been making a living from her writing since 1988, and since 2001 has written various novels: the highly acclaimed Charlie Fox series, including a prequel novella; standalone crime thrillers; and collaborations with espionage thriller author John Lawton, as well as numerous short stories. Her work has been used in Danish school textbooks, inspired an original song and music video, and been optioned for TV and film. Find out more at **www.ZoeSharp.com**

For Behind the Scenes, Bonus Features, Freebies, Sneak Peeks and advance notice of new stories, sign up for Zoë's **VIP list** at **www.ZoeSharp.com/vip-mailing-list**.

Zoë is always happy to hear from readers, reader groups, libraries or bookstores. You can contact her at **Zoe@ZoeSharp.com**

Visit Zoë's Amazon Author Page

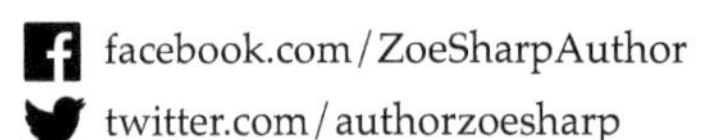

facebook.com/ZoeSharpAuthor
twitter.com/authorzoesharp
goodreads.com/authorzoesharp
amazon.com/author/zoesharp
instagram.com/authorzoesharp

ACKNOWLEDGEMENTS

Angela Norton
Derek Harrison
Dina Willner
Hazel Child
Hermann Schade
Jane Hudson, NuDesign
Jill Harrison
John Dowling
John Lawton
Matt Johnson
Pippa White
Robert Roper
Scott Clare
Tim Winfield

THE STORIES SO FAR...

*the **Charlie Fox** thrillers*

KILLER INSTINCT #1: Charlie Fox teaches women to defend themselves against rapists and murderers—just like the man who comes looking for her.

RIOT ACT #2: Charlie is supposed to be dog-sitting, not leading the resistance, but what else can a girl do when her housing estate turns into an urban battlefield?

HARD KNOCKS #3: Does Major Gilby's school in Germany specialise in training bodyguards—or killing them? When an old army comrade dies there, Charlie is sent undercover to find out.

Books 1–3 are also available as eBoxset #1

CHARLIE FOX: THE EARLY YEARS

FIRST DROP #4: Charlie's first bodyguard job in Florida should have been easy—until people start dying and she and her teenage charge are forced on the run.

ROAD KILL #5: When a motorcycle 'accident' almost kills her best friend, Charlie promises to find out what really happened. Even if that paints a huge target on her back.

SECOND SHOT #6: New England. A young child is in danger and Charlie will risk everything to keep her safe. But this time she's in no state to protect anyone, herself least of all.

Books 4–6 are also available as eBoxset #2

CHARLIE FOX: BODYGUARD

THIRD STRIKE #7: What's Charlie's worst nightmare? A 'bring your parents to work' day. When her surgeon father falls foul of a pharmaceutical giant, only Charlie stands in their way.

FOURTH DAY #8: A man joins the Fourth Day cult to prove they killed his son. By the time Charlie and Sean get him out, he's convinced otherwise. Then he dies...

FIFTH VICTIM #9: How can Charlie protect the daughter of a rich Long Island banker when the girl seems determined to put them both in harm's way?

DIE EASY #10: A deadly hostage situation in New Orleans forces Charlie to improvise as never before. And this time she can't rely on Sean to watch her back.

ABSENCE OF LIGHT #11: In the aftermath of an earthquake, Charlie's working alongside a team who dig out the living and ID the dead, and hoping they won't find out why she's *really* there.

FOX HUNTER #12: Charlie can never forget the men who put a brutal end to her army career, but she swore a long time ago she would never go looking for them. Now she doesn't have a choice.

BAD TURN #13: Charlie is out of work, out of her apartment and out of options. Why else would she be working for a shady arms dealer?

TRIAL UNDER FIRE #prequel: The untold story. Before she was a bodyguard, she was a soldier...

FOX FIVE RELOADED: short story collection. Charlie Fox. In small bites. With sharp teeth.

Where to Start?

If you enjoy reading about Charlie Fox right in the thick of it, working in close protection and travelling all over the world, I'd recommend you start with **FIRST DROP: #4**, or **CHARLIE FOX: BODYGUARD eBoxset #2**.

If, however, you want the full story of what happened to Charlie after she left the Army, and how she found her way into close protection, you'll want to start at the beginning, with **KILLER INSTINCT: #1**, or **CHARLIE FOX: THE EARLY YEARS eBoxset #1**.

*the **CSI Grace McColl and Detective Nick Weston** Lakes crime thrillers*

DANCING ON THE GRAVE: #1 A sniper with a mission, a CSI with something to prove, a young cop with nothing to lose, and a teenage girl with a terrifying obsession. The calm of the English Lake District is about to be shattered.

BONES IN THE RIVER: #2 Driving on a country road, late at night, you hit a child. There are no witnesses. You have *everything* to lose. What do you do?

standalone crime thrillers

THE BLOOD WHISPERER Six years ago CSI Kelly Jacks woke next to a butchered body with the knife in her hands and no memory of what happened. She trusted the evidence would prove her innocent. It didn't. Is history now repeating itself?

AN ITALIAN JOB (with **John Lawton**) Former soldiers Gina and Jack are about to discover that love is far deadlier the second time around.

*the **Blake & Byron** mystery thrillers*

THE LAST TIME SHE DIED (Oct 2021) She came back on the day of her father's funeral, ten years after she vanished. But she can't be who she says she is. Because we killed her. Didn't we?

Made in the USA
Middletown, DE
26 October 2023

41447428R00078